D1209193

GIRL WATCHER'S FUNERAL

Also by Hugh Pentecost

THE GIRL WITH SIX FINGERS
(A John Jericho Mystery)

THE GILDED NIGHTMARE
(A Pierre Chambrun Mystery)

DEAD WOMAN OF THE YEAR
(A John Jericho Mystery)

THE GOLDEN TRAP
(A Pierre Chambrun Mystery)

THE CREEPING HOURS
(A John Jericho Mystery)

THE EVIL THAT MEN DO
(A Pierre Chambrun Mystery)

HIDE HER FROM EVERY EYE
(A John Jericho Mystery)

SNIPER
(A John Jericho Mystery)

THE SHAPE OF FEAR
(A Pierre Chambrun Mystery)

ONLY THE RICH DIE YOUNG

THE TARNISHED ANGEL

THE CANNIBAL WHO OVERATE
(A Pierre Chambrun Mystery)

CHOICE OF VIOLENCE

THE DEADLY FRIEND

THE KINGDOM OF DEATH

THE LONELY TARGET

THE OBITUARY CLUB

THE ASSASSINS

CANCELLED IN RED

GIRL WATCHER'S FUNERAL

A PIERRE CHAMBRUN MYSTERY NOVEL

Hugh Pentecost

DODD, MEAD & COMPANY
NEW YORK

Library of Congress Catalog Card Number: 73-80709

Printed in the United States of America
by Vail-Ballou Press, Inc., Binghamton, N. Y.

Part One

1

I OFFER YOU a challenge.

You are to sit, relaxed and unperturbed, your legs casually crossed, your trousers neatly pressed, smoking your long, cool cigarette with an air of boredom while two of the most beautiful girls you ever laid eyes on parade before you wearing transparent evening gowns with absolutely nothing underneath the see-through chiffon and with only an ostrich ruffle circling their hips to conceal the complete woman. You are to view this with no more special interest than you would show the counterman who serves you your breakfast coffee and Danish at the corner coffee shop.

Maybe you could make it. I was trying, but I was certain that everyone in the Hotel Beaumont's Blue Lagoon Room, where the newest Paris designs were being modeled, could see that I was running a temperature.

"He's doing this because he likes diseases," a young voice

said at my elbow. "He's very fond of cancer, which is why he's doing it."

My head turned away from the two transparent models as though the hinge was rusty. A pale cloud of tobacco smoke swirled upward toward the concealed exhaust fans in the ceiling. A chamber music ensemble played softly on a raised platform at the far end of the room. There was the clink of glasses and subdued mutter of comment on the transparencies. I caught a glimpse of the elegant Mr. Cardoza, maitre d' of the Blue Lagoon Room, watching the waiters who circulated with silver trays of hot and cold hors d'oeuvres dreamed up by Mr. Amato, the Beaumont's banquet manager, and executed with the artistic genius of Monsieur Pierre Fresney, the Beaumont's fabulous chef.

"In Paris he was fond of heart attacks," the young voice said. "That's why he did it in Paris."

I focused on the owner of the voice, fighting the urge to take one more look at the transparent models before they turned their backs on me and retreated up the runway. At any other time the owner of the voice would have had my instant, undivided attention. As it was, she managed it very quickly. I stood up and found myself looking levelly into her wide brown eyes. I am five feet eleven inches tall. I noticed she had on flat-heeled pumps—what I think are called clobber heels. She was wearing a beautifully cut black jump suit with kimono sleeves, tied at the waist with a wide, vivid-pink satin ribbon. Her hair was gold, done in a huge pony-tail knot at the nape of her graceful neck.

"Those nudies," she said, looking past me at the runway, "are by Monsieur X, whom everyone knows is Christian Dior, and they cost five hundred dollars. In Seventh Avenue chiffon they'll cost about eighty-nine dollars—and who would notice the difference?"

"On those girls," I said.

"That's what I mean, of course." She gave her pink satin ribbon a little flip with silver fingers. "This is a genuine Max Lazar. He gave it to me."

"Lazar?"

"No, silly. Nikos gave it to me." Her voice was husky, her smile wide, charming, young.

"Nikos?" I said, looking blank.

"Oh, my, I thought you knew who I was," she said. She laughed, and I felt a gentle waterfall of pleasure cascade down my spine. "We'd better start at the beginning. You're Mark Haskell—I hope—public relations director of the hotel. Yes?"

"Yes," I said.

"I'm Jan Morse," she said, "Nikos's secretary—sort of."

"Sort of?"

"I mean I don't type—and things," she said.

"I can see that would be a waste," I said. I looked across the room, crowded with New York's high society, whatever that is, to where a huge man sat in a huge armchair drinking a huge glass of milk and watching the two transparencies disappear backstage. I had been a little slow on the uptake with Miss Morse. There is only one "Nikos"—Nikos Karados. All rich Greeks are said to be in the shipping business, but there weren't enough ships on all the oceans to account for the Karados fortune. Karados was a very special guest of the Beaumont's at the moment, and it was part of my job to report to his suite each morning at nine-thirty to find out if he had anything in mind that needed public relations treatment. The "secretary" had never been in evidence on my morning visits.

Karados was monstrous. I mean big, like three hundred and fifty pounds. He was taller than I, but his huge girth made him look short and squat. He dressed in a rather conservative fashion except for gaudy diamond and emerald rings worn on both pudgy hands. His small bright eyes were set in deep pouches wrinkled by years and years of laughter. I imagined he could be a very tough cookie if he was crossed, but I'd never seen him other than bubbling with good humor. He was as bald as a large egg, and when he smiled, which was continuously, there were bright patches of gold. But you treated this semi-comic man with deep respect. He could buy the hotel if he didn't like the way his eggs were poached. Beyond that he was an old friend of Pierre Chambrun's. Chambrun is my boss, the—I think it's safe to say—world-famous resident manager of the Beaumont, New York's top luxury hotel. Chambrun will take umbrage at that. "The world's top luxury hotel," he would tell you, "unique and unsurpassed. Perhaps, in outer space—!" He would shrug at this remote possibility.

"Nikos is very, very fond of cancer," Jan Morse said, her brown eyes narrowed as she inspected a new model who came out on the runway wearing a delightfully simple-looking evening gown. My program told me it was "of apricot double-faced gabardine; taut bodice with very cutout round armholes; high in back with a scooped-out front; enormous full skirt. All bias." Oh, well!

"You've said twice that Karados is very fond of cancer," I said to Jan Morse. "What the hell are you talking about?"

"You goose," she said. "Don't you know that everyone in this room, except the working stiffs like you and me and the waiters, has paid five hundred dollars a ticket to get in to see these creations? And it all goes to the cancer fund because Nikos is very fond of the cancer fund. All the expenses come out of his pocket—the model fees, the food and drink, the rent of the hall—so that every cent people have paid in goes to cancer."

I did a rapid calculation and guessed that Nikos was about ten thousand bucks out of pocket for the rent of the hall, the liquor and food, the service, the music, the models. I realized that this hurt him about as much as a twenty-cent tip to a shoeshine boy hurt me. I decided he might as well buy me another dry martini, and I signaled to a passing waiter. I guessed there were five hundred paying customers in the room, which meant the cancer fund was doing very well indeed.

A few days from now, I knew, all these people could get in here without paying a cent to see the exclusive showing of Max Lazar's new spring *haute couture*. They could get in without paying a cent *if*—if they had an invitation. Without an invitation God wouldn't be able to get in. And how would one go about getting an invitation? One would have to apply to Nikos Karados, Max Lazar's patron and financial backer. It would be unfortunate if it mattered to you to be present for the Lazar showing—and I knew it was vitally important to a great many in society, in the trade—if you had ever made any unflattering comments about the size of Nikos's tummy, or the flashes of gold in his smile, or the curious collection of friends who enjoyed the hospitality of his yacht. Getting in to see Max Lazar's collection would have the world of high fashion panting with anxiety.

As a professional public relations man I had to admire Nikos as an operator—Nikos or someone on his staff. By being here today you made a public display of your bank account. By being here for the Lazar showing, a privilege you couldn't buy, the world of fashion would know that you were "in." To some people that could be of life-and-death importance.

"Oh, my God, he's having another one!" Jan Morse cried out and started to run in and out of tables toward the giant fat man in the giant armchair.

Nikos Karados was slumping down in his chair, like a massive landslide, clutching at his chest. A woman screamed. The imperturbable model in the apricot all-bias evening gown picked up her long skirt and galloped back along the runway toward oblivion.

I was right behind Jan and I saw Mr. Cardoza making a sharp signal to waiters to clear the area. I didn't shout at him to call Dr. Partridge, the house physician. I knew he'd already done it.

Nikos Karados, fear in his little eyes, had slid down to a sitting position on the floor.

"My—my vest pocket," he muttered in a voice that sounded like a man gargling.

It was Jan's silver-tipped fingers that produced the little green glass vial from Nikos's pocket and unscrewed the cap. She emptied a white pill into the palm of her hand.

"Here, darling—quick—it's going to be all right," she said. She tilted back his head and I could see her place the pill under his tongue. "There, there," Jan crooned at him.

For a moment the fat man seemed to relax, and then his panic-filled eyes turned to me. "Dear God," he whispered. "It doesn't work!" He rolled over onto his back, his eyes closed, fluttering.

I felt flooded by all the perfumes of Araby as New York's best-dressed women tried to crowd in. I heard Mr. Cardoza's voice, cool and commanding.

"Mouth-to-mouth, Mr. Haskell," he said.

Most of us on the hotel staff have been trained in first aid. But it wasn't I who got to Karados. Jan Morse, in her beautiful black jump suit, was astride him, her lovely mouth pressed to his, trying to blow life into his lungs—oxygen that would keep the heart from stopping altogether.

"Come on, breathe, you sonofabitch," I heard myself saying.

The girl fought for him like a tiger. I was kneeling beside her.

"Want me to take over?" I asked

She shook her head.

And then Doc Partridge was there, his clean carbolic smell cutting through the heavy perfumes. He didn't stop Jan, but he rolled up Karados's sleeve and jabbed the fat arm with a hypodermic. Then and only then did he touch Jan's shoulder.

"I think you can stop that now, miss," he said.

Jan rose up, gasping for breath. Unexpectedly I felt her hand in mine as she tried to steady herself. I looked down at Karados and saw the dark eyelids fluttering. He was still alive. Partridge—old, white, cantankerous—watched, sniffing at a handful of pills from the little green vial.

Then Karados opened his eyes and found himself looking at Doc Partridge. His thick lips moved in a wry smile. "You old quack," he whispered. "Your medicine didn't work."

And then he died, his moon face twisted by a final agony. . . .

Sudden death is not the rarest of happenings at the Beaumont. The great hotel is like a small city within itself, with its own mayor, its own police force, its own hospital, library, shops, restaurants, bars, convention areas, day nursery school, scores of employees doing dozens and dozens of specialized jobs. There are the hundreds of rooms where people live for short or long periods of time, and on the top floors there are about a dozen co-op apartments and penthouses, actually owned by the tenants but serviced by the hotel. Elderly people and not-so-elderly people die of heart attacks at a ratio that may be slightly higher than that of the average small town. Overdrinking and overeating and overindulgence in sex may be a little more the order of the day at the Beaumont than in your home town. Several times a year I am involved in covering up the fact that some old goat has died in the bedroom of a young woman who was, almost certainly, not his wife.

The death of Nikos Karados would, I knew, provide the news media with a ball. Nikos had been in the public eye for forty years. He was Greek by birth, but I honestly didn't know what country would claim him as a citizen. His stamping grounds had been Rome and Florence, the French Riviera and Paris, London, New York, Acapulco. His huge fortune, accumulated God knows how, had first been involved with ships, and then with commercial aviation, with films, with the cosmetics industry, and most recently with high fashion. All these ventures seemed to be games to Nikos, not businesses. But whatever motivated Nikos, the results were always the same. Like Midas, whatever he touched multiplied in value, turned to gold. If he supported a charity, it flourished. If he helped a friend with a loan to start a business, that business was bound to succeed, even though Nikos had no direct involvement. Most very rich men have a sort of sinister aura floating in their backgrounds; Nikos had always been a smiling Santa Claus with a never-empty pack on his back.

I knew it had not all been play. Nikos's friendship with my boss, Pierre Chambrun, dated back to a dark time when Chambrun was fighting in the French Resistance. Nikos, relaxing at his Swiss estate, had actually been pouring money into the Resistance, helping them to buy arms and munitions and explosives. He had, it seemed, a small but highly efficient espionage force at his command that kept Chambrun and his fighters constantly aware of the next Nazi move. Nikos, smiling his golden smile and passing out lollipops to Swiss children, had actually been a grim fighter in the cause of freedom. Chambrun would regret his passing.

The girl who still clung to my hand as the Blue Lagoon Room was cleared of fashion experts and Nikos's huge body, covered by a sheet, was lifted onto a hospital stretcher from our emergency room and wheeled away, wept unashamedly.

"He was so kind, so generous, so—so very compassionate," she said.

"Obviously this wasn't his first attack," I said.

"Oh, no," Jan said. "There have been a half dozen others. He knew that someday the pills wouldn't work. He wasn't afraid to die."

Except at the last moment, I thought. I had seen fear in his eyes, and yet his last words had been a wisecrack at Doc Partridge.

"Is there anything I can do for you, Jan?" I asked. "Can I take you up to your room? Because there are many things about this that involve my job. The news people must be notified. And I assume the whole business of Max Lazar's showing day after tomorrow will have to go down the drain."

"Oh, no!" Jan said. "Nikos never left anything to chance—the chance that he would die before some project he was interested in was completed. You'll find that Tim has all the instructions for carrying on."

"Tim?"

"Tim Gallivan, Nikos's lawyer. You'll see, Mark. Money will have been specially set aside to carry out everything." She had managed to subdue the tears. "I'm all right. You don't have to worry about me. Except—"

"Except?"

"It's going to be awfully lonely later on. Perhaps, when you get untangled, you'd like to buy me a drink."

"It's a date," I said. "But it may be quite a while."

"My room is nineteen hundred seven," she said.

We started out toward the lobby together. Mr. Cardoza touched my arm.

"You're wanted in the Great Man's office," he said.

Chambrun, it seemed, was already aware of his friend's passing. . . .

Pierre Chambrun is a small dark man, stockily built, with heavy pouches under bright black eyes that can freeze the blood in your veins if you're guilty of some stupidity, or can unexpectedly twinkle with a kind of contagious humor. Born in France, he came to this country as a small child. He has been in the hotel business all his life, beginning as a shoeshine boy in the barbershop of an unpretentious East Side hotel run by an uncle. He has risen to the top of the heap as resident manager of the Beaumont.

I think Chambrun's genius as an executive lies in his ability to delegate authority, while at the same time being always close at hand to take full responsibility for touchy decisions. Every employee of the hotel is aware that by some unexplained magic Chambrun knows what's going on in a hundred different places at the same time. "When I don't know what's going on in my own hotel, it will be time for me to retire," he says. The Beaumont is his world. To him it is more than a highly efficient plant; it is a way of life.

Chambrun's private office on the second floor is not furnished like an office. The Oriental rug is priceless, a gift from an Indian maharaja who had been extricated from a romantic embarrassment by Chambrun. The flat-topped desk is Florentine, exquisitely carved. The high-backed chairs are also Florentine, beautiful to look at and unexpectedly comfortable. There is a sideboard by a far wall on which rests the paraphernalia of a coffee service and an ornate Turkish coffeemaker. There is a Blue Period Picasso on one wall, and a witty and impudent Chagall, replete with flying cows and a rooftop violinist, on another. There is no sign of office, no files, no visible safe; only the little intercom box on his desk which connects him with his secretary, Miss Ruysdale, in the outer office, and two telephones, one an unlisted private number and the other connected with the hotel switchboard.

Miss Ruysdale, smartly dressed, thirty-fivish, a fabulous woman about whom a whole book should be written someday, was at her desk when I arrived. She gave me her cool, somewhat distant smile.

"Hold onto your hat," she said.

"Now what?"

"Did he fall or was he pushed?" Miss Ruysdale said. "I think you'd better go in. I can hear his knuckles tapping the desk."

I opened the door to the inner sanctum. Chambrun was at his desk, sunk deep in his big armchair, hooded lids narrowing his eyes to two slits. Sitting opposite him, looking his usual cantankerous self, was Dr. Partridge.

Chambrun pointed at a little green bottle sitting on the desk in front of him. "You've seen this before, Mark?" he asked.

"Or one like it," I said. "Karados had it in his vest pocket."

"What did you see done with it?"

"Karados had his attack," I said. "I got to him with his secretary, a girl named Morse. He said something like '—in my vest pocket.' Jan found it, and—"

"Jan?"

"Miss Morse."

"You know her well, then?"

"Just met her three minutes before it happened," I said.

"I see. So Miss Morse found the bottle. What did she do?"

"Opened it, took out a pill, and slipped it under Karados's

tongue." I sensed trouble. "Something wrong with that?"

"Perfectly correct procedure," Partridge said.

"So?"

"So Karados looked at me after a few seconds and said, 'Dear God. It doesn't work!' Then I heard Cardoza suggest mouth-to-mouth. Before I could move, Jan—Miss Morse—was giving it to him. She fought like a madwoman for him. You saw that, Doctor."

"Why are you defensive about her?" Chambrun asked.

"Look here, Mr. Chambrun, why don't you come clean with me?" I said. "You suspect something?"

Chambrun made a little gesture to Partridge.

The old doctor cleared his throat. "Karados had angina," he said. "The pills he took when he had an attack were nitroglycerine. This particular supply I prescribed for him. Made up in the hotel drugstore."

"So this time they didn't work," I said.

"Damn right they didn't work," Partridge said. "They didn't work because what's in that bottle now are soda mints —bicarbonate."

"They would kill him?"

"Yes, they'd kill him," Partridge said angrily, "because they wouldn't do anything for him. Harmless, but of no use whatever to a man in the throes of an angina attack. Whoever replaced those nitro tablets with soda mints might just as well have shot Karados through the heart."

"You or the pharmacist made a mistake," I suggested.

"Don't be an ass!" Partridge said.

"So you call the police," I said.

Chambrun didn't answer at once. He'd taken his silver cigarette case out of the breast pocket of his coat and was tapping one of his flat Egyptian cigarettes on it. Finally he lit it.

"Between ourselves," he said. "Nikos Karados was very

close to me at a time when friendship and loyalty were at a premium. I would not like to let him down, even in death. Now there are two possibilities before us. Someone close to Nikos—close enough to have access to a bottle that would never be out of his reach— Am I right about that, Doctor?"

"A man with angina would carry those nitro pills on him wherever he went," Partridge said. "At night they'd be no further from him than his bedside table."

Chambrun nodded. "So someone very close to him managed to get hold of that bottle for long enough to flush the nitro pills down the john and replace them with soda mints. That's one possibility. The second is suicide. Nikos was ready to die; he made sure that when the moment came he couldn't change his mind."

"You buy that?" Partridge asked.

"No," Chambrun said. "I never knew a man who relished every moment of living, important or unimportant, as much as Nikos. He ran risks all his life. German intelligence tried to assassinate him half a dozen times during World War Two. Nikos fought to live. Suicide is unthinkable. He was always having too much fun."

"So you call the police," I said again.

Chambrun ignored me. He pressed the intercom button on his desk and Miss Ruysdale's voice came through, cool and clear.

"Yes, Mr. Chambrun?"

"Be good enough to bring me a chart of all the Karados accommodations as they stand at the moment, please." Chambrun leaned back in his chair and looked at the curl of gray ash on the end of his cigarette. It reached the silver ash tray on his desk just as it was falling. "You know much about high fashion, Mark?" he asked.

"I read Marylin Bender's column in the *Times*," I said. "I

glance at *Women's Wear Daily*. I know who Baby Jane Holser is, thanks to Tom Wolfe. I mean, the fashion columnists have taken over from the society columnists."

"Rather superficial, I'd say," Chambrun said. "We are, for the moment, the fashion center of the world, thanks to Nikos. I had some misgivings about involving the Beaumont, but Nikos pointed out to me that if you can hold a fashion show in the Metropolitan Museum of Art twice a year, the Beaumont shouldn't flinch at the idea. And he was Nikos, my friend. The nineteenth floor is, at the moment, a pop-fashion jungle, as nearly as I can make out—designer, models, models' agents, photographers, columnists, stylists, public relations geniuses, the boy friends of beautiful girls, the girl friends of beautiful girls—God knows who else. Nikos was the center of it all, paying for it all, bent on turning Max Lazar from a comparatively unknown designer into the big guru of mod-fashion. These people are in and out of each other's rooms, including Nikos's suite, like one big, uninhibited family; incest to Beatle music. It is one long, swinging party planned to last until after Lazar's showing day after tomorrow. Only the models are kept on a leash. They must not have bloodshot eyes or that tired look when they come out on the runway wearing Lazar's concoctions."

"You're saying too damn many people could have had access to that little green bottle," Partridge said.

"Thanks for your concise brevity, Doctor," Chambrun said.

Partridge stood up. "What you do about all this is your affair, Pierre. I have signed the death certificate. No medical hanky-panky. He died of angina pectoris. The fact that he didn't take a nitro pill has no medical significance as far as cause of death is concerned. He died of natural–unnatural causes. If you'll excuse me, I'm late for a game of cribbage in the Spartan Bar."

"Thank you, Doctor—I think," Chambrun said. "I'd be happier if you hadn't been so observant about the pills. As it is—" He lifted his shoulders in a Gallic shrug.

The doctor passed Miss Ruysdale in the office door. She came in as he went out and placed a sheet of paper on Chambrun's desk.

"Karados is in Suite Nineteen–A," she said, pointing to the paper. "Adjoining it on the north is nineteen hundred one, occupied by Timothy Gallivan, Karados's lawyer and financial adviser. On the south is nineteen hundred seven, occupied by one Jan Morse, listed as Karados's secretary. There are connecting doors from both these rooms with Karados's suite—keys on the Karados side of the door. Down the hall are four models, most notably Suzie Sands, top high-fashion model in the business. There is Monica Strong, the stylist who will stage-manage Lazar's showing. There is Lazar himself. There is Michael Faraday, millionaire girl watcher, and his glamorous wife, known as Dodo."

"Girl watching is everybody's thing," I said. Nobody seemed to be listening.

"Suzie Sands is registered as Mrs. Thomas Tryon," Miss Ruysdale said. "Tommy Tryon shares her room with her. Off the record, they are not married, Mr. Chambrun. Believe it or not, Suzie is putting Tommy through law school. At a hundred and fifty dollars an hour for her modeling talents she can well afford it."

"You are a mine of information, Ruysdale," Chambrun said.

"Any time, Mr. Chambrun. In passing, Mr. Timothy Gallivan is in my office waiting to see you. He is—"

"Nikos's lawyer," Chambrun said. "Hang onto him till I buzz you. Get word to Jerry Dodd that I want to see him."

Jerry Dodd is the hotel's security officer. We don't have a "house detective" at the Beaumont.

Miss Ruysdale went out, and Chambrun sat staring at the little green bottle. I thought for a moment he'd forgotten that I was still there. He hadn't.

"This bottle," he said, "was certainly handled by Nikos when he put it in his vest pocket, by Miss Morse when she took it out, and by Partridge—before he knew there might be anything wrong with it. Therefore, no meaningful fingerprints." He looked at me, his eyes narrowed. "If the police come into the picture, we lose the game before it starts. There is no physical evidence. The nitro pills are certainly gone. A five-year-old child could buy soda mints without question. Inject a cop into the picture and everyone sits tight and nothing happens. There is just one chance to get at the truth, Mark. We have two days in which to listen, circulate, and watch. It's just possible that someone a little high, a little overstimulated, may let something slip. I'll get in touch with our friend Lieutenant Hardy at Homicide and tell him the score. I think he'll agree that the best procedure is to let us handle it for the next couple of days."

"It sounds reasonable," I said. "If anybody can come up with anything, Jerry Dodd is the boy."

"Not Jerry, Mark," Chambrun said, shaking his head. "A security officer will arouse suspicions. The one person free to come and go without being at all obvious is the hotel's public relations man. They'll welcome you because they welcome every possible shred of publicity."

"Me!" I said.

"You," Chambrun said. He smiled faintly. "Your three-minute friendship with Miss Morse seems like a good opening wedge."

I just stared at him.

"You and I, Ruysdale, Jerry Dodd, and the Doctor are the only ones who'll know what's in the wind. To the rest of the world Nikos died of angina. Period. Understood?"

"Yes, sir," I said in a small voice.

His smile widened slightly. "I'm sure you've always wanted to play cops and robbers, Mark." Then the smile disappeared. "I count on you. Nikos was my good friend."

"Yes, sir."

"Now, shall we see what Mr. Gallivan has on his mind?"

2

I SUPPOSE I should have expected that Timothy Gallivan would be something rather special. Karados wouldn't have had an intimate he trusted with all his affairs who was ordinary. Gallivan was short and lithe, and he seemed to be full of bounce, as though at any moment he might take off in a soft-shoe routine. I was reminded of an old movie I'd seen on the Late-Late show—Jimmy Cagney playing the role of George M. Cohan in *Yankee Doodle Dandy*. Gallivan had that kind of irrepressible energy that made both Cagney and Cohan great performers. His smile was ready to explode at you any second. I imagined that he and Nikos had spent a lot of time laughing together at the cockeyed world.

"I don't know much about Greek wakes," Gallivan said, when he'd introduced himself, "but Nikos wasn't having any. Cremation at once—and a party. That was his idea. Always leave them laughing. Would you believe there's money—a hell of a lot of money—set aside in a dozen places to buy drinks for friends when the moment came: the Ritz in Paris, Moriarty's Saloon here in New York, Sardi's, Dinty Moore's, The House of Chan, some dump in Athens, another in Rome, a London club where he was a member, a tailorshop in Dublin where he bought clothes, and here, Chambrun. For one hour, starting at the cocktail hour tomorrow, Nikos will pick up the whole tab in the Trapeze Bar. He wanted people to have fun on him."

"It's in character," Chambrun said.

"The reason I'm here," Gallivan said, rumpling his curly red hair that was salted here and there with gray, "is to reassure you about the fashion show. Everything will go on exactly as planned. The people involved who are registered here will stay on till after the showing. All the arrangements for the Blue Lagoon Room stand: the food, the liquor, the music." He chuckled. "A pop orchestra this time, Chambrun, that may send you screaming for some mountaintop. But Nikos wanted it; something in the mod-mood. There are no problems about prompt payment. Nikos knew this was going to happen someday. Money for this brawl is in a special account to which I have immediate access."

"I wasn't worried," Chambrun said.

Gallivan's smile faded and he shook his head. "It's going to be a strange world without him," he said. "Twenty years I've been at his elbow, night and day. Never a dull moment. I am suddenly so rich I couldn't count it if I wanted to. I'd gladly give it all back just to have him walk in that door." His bright blue eyes lifted to fix on Chambrun. "You knew him when it counted."

"Yes, when it counted heavily," Chambrun said.

"I knew him then, but I didn't become permanently involved with him until nineteen fifty." Gallivan drew a deep breath and grinned at us. "Well, my one aim now is to make these next three days the success Nikos wanted them to be. Did you know, gentlemen, that *Women's Wear* has not paid proper attention to Max Lazar? Did you know that the high priestesses of the fashion world have not bowed deeply to Lazar? Did you know that a fat Greek shipping tycoon intended to kick these lady fashion writers and their rag-trade bible in their respective smug rumps and catapult Mr. Lazar over their prostrate forms to the top of the high-fashion mountain? That's what Nikos meant to do, just for the hell of it, you understand, and by God, that's what we'll all do for him. This show here at the Beaumont is just the beginning. But it will be a shot heard round the world!"

"You say 'we'll do it for him,'" Chambrun said. "Who is 'we,' Mr. Gallivan?"

"The team," Gallivan said. "There was a 'team' in your time, Chambrun—the people who kept you and your Resistance people informed. That's how Nikos worked. A team for each project—a team of specialists. We have them now. The team includes me—handling the money whip; Monica Strong, a stylist who will stage a show that will leave them breathless; Zach Chambers, who can produce the most beautiful models in the world, exclusively for us; the Michael Faradays, who will provide us with the society tie-in we must have; and there is Rosemary Lewis, fashion columnist who will die laughing as she whizzes past the opposition. And there is, of course, Max Lazar, who has designed the product."

"Is he any good?" Chambrun asked.

Gallivan gave us another candid grin. "How good is good?" he asked. "He is talented. He is a disciple of the cult of pop-fashion. Is he a put-on? Is he just plain mod-camp? That's for you to decide, gentlemen. But the final answer to this little skirmish is who blows the loudest trumpet. I've got a few million bucks that says we will!" His laughter was full of delight. "You want the girls to put on underwear again? When we're through, if Lazar says so, they will. You like girls without bras, or do you prefer the No Bra Bra? It will be Lazar who determines the future of the female bosom, not a trade paper or a fashion writer."

"Is Jan Morse a member of the team?" I asked.

The blue eyes turned my way and I thought for a second a glacial hardness covered them. Then he laughed. "The general must never be allowed to become bored," he said, "or he may lose interest and the battle be lost. Jan is a darling girl with the mind of a twelve-year-old and the instincts of a Lolita. It pleased Nikos just to look at her. She kept the general from being bored. She is now, though she doesn't know it yet, a very rich and desirable young heiress."

The key, I remembered, had been on Nikos's side of the door. I felt unaccountably depressed.

"It's my job at the moment," Gallivan said, "to rally the team. We are holding a slight drinking bash in Nikos's suite. Nikos's wish. 'Not later than an hour after my death the people closest to me will meet to eat and drink and remember happily all the past joys of our time together.' His words. You gentlemen are both cordially invited."

"Unfortunately I'm up to my neck in problems," Chambrun said, "but I'm sure Mark will accept with pleasure. It's his job to cover the public relations aspect of this whole affair for the Beaumont."

"Come along, chum," Gallivan said to me. "If nothing else, you will get a glimpse of some women that will make your young mouth water."

I looked at Chambrun. His face was innocently blank. . . .

Under normal circumstances if anyone had suggested to me that I'd enjoy going somewhere to watch girls, I'd have had a stock reply. "Why should I want to watch girls? I've got a girl." It just happened, however, that Nikos Karados had chosen a disturbed time in my private life to die. I have a fabulous secretary, golden blond, shaped like a lewd angel, witty and full of fire, named Shelda Mason. For two years Shelda and I have lived a very happy, totally involved, life together. We both have what Shelda calls "Chambrun fever." The Beaumont is our joint life. I have a suite of rooms on the fourth floor, down the hall from my office, and Shelda has a small garden apartment two blocks from the hotel on the East Side. I keep clothes in both places.

Shelda and I had come to an unexpected crossroad. We could go on forever, without any sort of permanent obligation to each other, loving every minute of it; or we could take the plunge, tie the knot, make it final, total. It sounds like a simple decision to make, but somehow it wasn't. I think we were both a little afraid to change the status of our relationship. It might not be as wonderfully good, as free and as completely fun.

It so happened that Chambrun had some rather special business to transact with Mr. George Battle, owner of the Beaumont, who sits in the sun on the French Riviera counting his money. Chambrun, who had never told anything about our relationship and knew everything about it, suggested that Shelda might act as his courier. She would spend a couple of weeks on the Riviera and in Paris doing some odds and ends for him, buy herself some new clothes, have herself a ball.

It seemed to make sense. Separated for a couple of weeks, Shelda and I might come to some kind of decision about ourselves. For two weeks, Shelda said on the night before she left, we'd both be completely free. If I found myself interested in another girl, I was to be unhampered, and no recriminations. If she found herself intrigued, same deal. I knew, of course, that no other girl was going to interest me, but I felt a hot iron turning in my gut when I thought of Shelda and some other man. I daresay she felt the same thing. I was to meet Shelda ten days from now at Kennedy, with or without a marriage license in my pocket. She would say yes or no. There'd be no discussions, no regrets. The moment of final decision would take place then.

That was the state of my emotional life when I headed for Gallivan's drinking bash in the late Nikos Karados's suite on the 19th floor. I could be girl-watcher without feeling guilty, I assured myself. Actually it would have to be just in passing. My job was to sniff out some kind of lead to a particularly subtle killer who might also be girl watching.

The Beaumont's suites and rooms are soundproofed by experts. When I walked along the 19th floor corridor, it was as quiet as St. Patrick's Cathedral. When the door of 19A was opened in answer to my buzz, I was nearly knocked over on my back by a wave of sound—loud voices, music, slightly drunken laughter. An astonishing redhead with green eye shadow and a skirt that came a good four inches below her hip bones grabbed me by the front of my dark blue blazer, pulled me into the room, and gave me a full and very active kiss on the mouth.

"Welcome!" she shouted at me, when she'd finished working me over. Then she laughed as she saw me reaching for my handkerchief. I had to be smeared with that scarlet lipstick. "You're safe, baby," she said. "It doesn't come off. A House of Lazar special."

Well, that was one way to promote a product.

No two suites at the Beaumont are decorated in identical style. Nineteen–A has dark green brocade walls with a Flemish painting or two strategically placed. It is usually reserved for the very rich and the slightly old-fashioned. Nikos Karados, despite his mod contacts, was fond of it and had always asked for it over the years. It was far from being the correct setting for the current production.

A young man in tight pants, a Nehru jacket, a string of coral beads around his neck, strutted past me, jabbing a finger at me and chanting, "Here come de judge! Here come de judge!"

There were girls in very chic see-through black lace, there was one in a camellia-pink pants suit, and another in black satin pants with a white silk turtle-neck blouse and a little black bolero. I saw Mrs. Michael Faraday in a handsome dark brocade embroidered, no less, with rhinestone snowflakes. Pants and ersatz jewelry and see-through tops or flesh-colored tops that looked like skin seemed to be the order of the day. And the men—if they were men! Max Lazar, standing over by the fireplace sipping a martini on the rocks in a huge glass, had set the pattern. His hair was long, growing down into his open collar, his pants were tight-fitting, made of a shiny black material, and his white shirt was open to the base of his hairless chest. On his bare feet were black patent leather evening pumps. There was a cowboy vest made out of what looked like sable. There were more Nehru jackets, and turtle necks, and beads everywhere. I saw Tim Gallivan coming toward me, armed with two martinis. He'd changed from his conservative business suit into blue chino slacks, a navy turtleneck sweater, brown loafers on his bare feet.

"Every inch the Southampton croquet player," a pleasant female voice, cultivated, said at my elbow.

You couldn't speak softly in the room because of all the laughter and screaming and the two boys in the far corner with Beatle hairdos working on a guitar and a set of blood-red drums.

Gallivan reached me and handed me one of the martinis. He introduced me to the lady who'd just finished describing him.

"Monica Strong—Mark Haskell," he said. "You two should get to know each other. Monica's the gal who's staging the Lazar showing, Mark. She'll be coming to you for help along the way."

"Pleasure," I said.

Monica Strong did not belong to that fifty percent of the world which is twenty-five or under. Without meaning to downgrade her in this mod society, I guessed she was in her late thirties or early forties. She had on a very chic beige jersey suit with a wine-red blouse. There was a floppy bow at her neck. She had the legs for the short skirt. But with this one you didn't look at the clothes first. She had a really beautiful face—classic in structure: high cheekbones with little hollows below them, a wide, generous mouth, and candid gray-green eyes under long black lashes. Her hair was a shiny bird-wing black, quantities of it done in a very elegant bouffant coiffure. For my money she outshone all the groovy kids in the room, even the glamorous Mrs. Faraday.

"I've been wanting to find you, Mark," she said, "but things are on the hectic side. There are details I need to work out with you."

"Any time, anyplace," I said.

Gallivan had drifted away, leaving me with the lady and my bathtub of gin. The stomping and shouting to the music seemed to grow louder.

"You have enough models here to show three designers' collections," I said.

Her smile was enchanting, if just a touch bitter. "About

half of these gals aren't models," she said. "Fashion has become a Barnum and Bailey world, Mark. Everyone gets into the act, particularly the young matrons in the high-fashion world. The nuder the look, the surer you can be that they aren't professional models."

I took a sip of my drink. It was dynamite. "I wonder how Nikos would have enjoyed this?" I said.

A shadow crossed the lovely face, and for just an instant some sort of guard was lowered and she looked wounded, hurt.

"Nikos resented age," she said. "Contributing to the insanities of these groovy young people delighted him. He thought they were utterly mad, but he loved them. Yes, he'd have enjoyed it."

I glanced toward the bedroom door. The traffic in and out of there was just as heavy as it was in the living room. "I haven't seen the little secretary about," I said.

Monica looked at me, an elegant eyebrow raised. "Secretary?"

"Jan," I said. "Jan Morse."

"Oh."

I grinned at her. "Oh what?" I said.

She laughed. "Oh damn!" she said. "I was being bitchy. Jan isn't one of my favorite people."

"She seemed pleasant, and harmless, and very genuinely concerned for Nikos. I was with her when it happened," I said.

The gray-green eyes looked at me steadily, the long lashes unblinking. "A man-eating shark probably looks pleasant and harmless—to other sharks," Monica said. "Shall we talk about something else, or would you like to circulate?"

She didn't give me any choice. She turned away and edged through the mob toward Max Lazar, who stood by the fireplace, dark and brooding, surrounded by a platoon of young and very exposed wives of older and very rich, not-present husbands.

I headed, glass in hand, toward the bedroom. The scene there was different. It was crowded and hot and noisy, but very In. A campy-looking gray-haired man wearing gold beads over a pink turtle-neck sweater was telling dirty stories. Propped up against the pillows on the huge double bed where Nikos Karados had slept last night were a pair of identical twins. They had mahogany-red hair worn in long bobs. They had on black velvet pants suits, their long legs stretched out in front of them, feet in black patent leather pumps. Their white shirts were frilly lace at the collars and cuffs. They were holding hands. It took me a moment to realize that one was a girl and one was a boy. The court jester, the old camp in the beads, was directing his performance at the couple on the bed.

"Suzie darling, have you heard the one about the television comic who came face to face with Merle Oberon on the beach at Acapulco?"

The girl twin opened her mouth and spoke. She should never have done it. Her voice was high, flat—awful.

"Tell us, Zach dear," she said. It was enough to end all illusion of glamor.

I realized this must be Suzie Sands, the top high-fashion model in the business. Her fee for being photographed in the great clothes was a hundred and fifty dollars an hour. The look-alike young man must be her Tommy whom she was putting through law school. I wondered if he wore his beads to class.

I wasn't particularly interested in the story about the TV comic and Merle Oberon. I edged over to the door that I knew led to Room 1907. The key was on this side. I turned it, opened the door, and went through it.

The room is a single with a small entrance alcove and a bathroom with a black marble tub built close to the floor like a swimming pool.

Jan Morse, still wearing the elegant black jump suit with the pink ribbon at her wasp waist, was flat out on the bed, hands locked behind her golden head. Stretched over her eyes was what looked like a wet washcloth.

I closed the door, trying to make noise.

"I thought you'd never come," Jan said. She reached up and took the cloth from her eyes. She'd obviously been trying to reduce the slight puffiness produced by tears. When she saw me, she sat up. "Oh, it's you," she said.

"You were expecting maybe Richard Burton?" I said. "You invited me, remember?"

"Not without knocking," she said. "I don't know you that well—yet."

With the door to the Karados suite closed, the silence was deafening. I took a sip of my martini and watched the girl on the bed. She had pulled her knees up under her chin, wrapped her arms around her legs, and was staring back at me like a concentrated thinker. "The mind of a twelve-year-old and the instincts of a Lolita," Gallivan had said.

"The key was on the other side of the door," I said, "so I thought—"

"I know what you thought," she said. She swung around and dropped her legs over the edge of the bed. They were long legs, lovely legs, and the stockings were so sheer and so exactly the color of her bronzed skin that I wouldn't have been sure she was wearing any if I hadn't seen the panty-tops while she was sitting up on the bed. "Can I have a sip of your drink?" she asked.

"Sure. I'll go back and get you one of your own if you say the word."

"I might lock the door on you," she said.

"Then the person you were expecting couldn't get in," I said.

"You're a smart schmuk," she said.

"A little while ago you chose me to help out with your loneliness," I said. I handed her my martini jug, still half full.

She took a very ladylike swallow and handed it back. "That was yesterday," she said.

"That was an hour ago."

"An hour ago is yesterday," she said. "An hour ago is a year ago—Deadsville. Lived through and dead."

"All right, let's begin with now," I said. "Can I help with your loneliness until the person you're expecting arrives?"

"Do whatever you damn please," she said. She got up and walked over to the window which overlooked the East River. She stood with her back to me, staring out at the early evening darkness. After a moment she spoke to me without turning. "How well do you know that old quack?" she asked.

"What old quack?"

"You know a lot of old quacks?" She turned, and the brown eyes were wide and dilated. "The doctor back there when Nikos had his Thing."

"Dr. Partridge? I know him well."

"He killed Nikos, you know."

I felt, suddenly, very wide awake. "You're off your rocker," I said. "What do you mean he killed him?"

"Those pills were no good," Jan said. "Oh, I don't mean if they had been Nikos mightn't have died. But he didn't react at all. And there was no odor to them. I was giving him mouth-to-mouth, you know—and there was like nothing."

"You've given him mouth-to-mouth before when he'd had an attack?"

"No, but I've been around him when he took nitro. You

could smell it on his breath. That old quack crossed him up with something that was nothing."

"It should be very easy to check out," I said. "The drugstore that filled the prescription is right here in the hotel."

"They'd cover up for the old quack." She turned back to the window. "You know what?"

"What?"

"Nikos was murdered," she said without turning. "That's why I couldn't go to the party—to celebrate a murder." She turned around. "Well, why aren't you screaming a defense of your killer friend?"

I drained my martini glass and put it down on the center table. "I'm winded," I said.

"You don't believe it?"

"If there was anything wrong with those pills, Jan, it wasn't Doc Partridge's doing," I said. "That I'd swear to."

"And I can't prove it," she said. "The Doc took the bottle away with him. What if I went to the police? So they ask your old quack for the bottle and the right pills are in it now. End of investigation. And maybe I can get sued—or something." She turned away again. "You know why I'd been crying when you came in?"

"Because you were sad about Nikos."

"Because I was so goddam mad at the goddam frustrating position I'm in," she said. "I can't prove anything and yet I *know!*"

It had happened just a little too fast for me to be sure what league I was playing in. She had the facts upside-down, but she was right about the core of the truth. Someone had made certain Nikos wouldn't survive his next angina attack.

My mouth felt dry. "Have you thought of the possibility that someone else might have shifted pills on Nikos? Because, seriously, you can count Doc Partridge out. He's old, but he's top-flight."

The brown eyes narrowed.

"I mean, if the pills were shifted," I said.

"Whatever those pills were, I tell you they weren't nitro," she said. "I would have smelled them on his breath."

Well I knew they hadn't been nitro, so she was right about that.

"What you're saying doesn't make any sense," she said. "How could anybody have shifted the pills? Nikos always carried them in his vest pocket. He wouldn't have walked across the room without them. They were the difference to him between living and dying—and I can tell you, Mark, Nikos didn't want to die."

"What about at night—when he went to bed?"

"He kept them on the bedside table." Then she exploded. "You stinker!" she said. "You think I spent my nights with him?"

"Did you?" I said. "If you open up a murder investigation, it's a question that'll be asked, Jan."

"Damn you!" she said.

"Just what were your duties as secretary? You say you didn't type—clerical work?"

"I was his appointment secretary," she said. "I kept track of who he had to see—and like when."

"He had access to this room," I said. "Key on his side of the door."

"He didn't sleep very well," she said. "Fits and starts, sort of. If he had an idea in the middle of the night, he'd come in and wake me up."

"An idea about appointments?"

"I think I've decided you are a nasty jerk!" she said.

"You brought all this up, not I," I said. "Let's get back to the pill bottle on his bedside table. You spent your nights here, waiting for him to get ideas. Who spent time in the other room with him?"

"The key was on his side of the door," she said. "These rooms are soundproofed. You ought to know that. You work here."

"I'll bet you're a wonderful guesser," I said.

"I think I'd like it if you went back to the party," she said.

"Let me make something quite clear to you, baby," I said. "If Nikos went to Doc Partridge for a prescription for nitro pills, that's what he got. If the pills in the bottle when he had his attack weren't nitro, then somebody shifted them. If you go to the police and open up this can of peas, you're going to be asked all these questions by someone who'll demand answers. And everyone else who was close to Nikos will be asked questions about him, about you, and about anyone else who was close to him. I'm not being a jerk. I want to help. Who are the very close ones who would come and go in Nikos's bedroom?"

I could see her struggling with a decision. I watched her, thinking Chambrun would be pleased with the way I was handling things. She'd opened the door for me to ask questions I couldn't have asked on my own.

"It wasn't just nighttime," Jan said.

"How's that?"

"He spent a lot of time propped up in bed in there—holding court, you might say. People came and went in droves. The hall door was left on the latch, so he wouldn't have to get up to open it if anybody knocked or rang. We all knew if the hall door was locked that he wasn't receiving." Her brown eyes, which had been averted, turned to me. "What you're thinking wasn't so, Mark. Sex was a thing of the past with Nikos. Because of his heart—well, he was afraid. I mean—well, that's what I mean."

"Suppose you try saying all of what you mean," I said.

She looked like a puzzled little child when that frown creased her forehead. "I've been with Nikos for almost two years," she said, "sleeping, most of the time, in a room right next to him or near him. So, if he had ideas he wanted to make notes on—well, like I told you. But in all that time, Mark, he never put a hand on me—except maybe a little pat on the shoulder if he helped me on with a coat or something. Nothing sexy; no mauling or pawing. And I never saw any dirty-old-Mansville routines with any of the other girls. He liked to have us around; he loved youth; I think he must have been a pretty lusty kid when he was young. But he wasn't young now. He didn't look it, you know, but he was seventy-five."

He hadn't looked any age, I thought; a great, fat Buddha.

"I think like it was maybe after his heart trouble started, which was long before me, that he got interested in women's fashions. It's not like the dressmaking business your hard-up aunt used to go into in the old days. It's a whole world in itself, you know?"

"Vaguely," I said.

"Oh, it's a great deal more than clothes and accessories—carefully matching dresses, cosmetics, and hairdos. It's what you do, and where you go and what you own. Women who make the fashion scene, like Dodo Faraday, are photographed in Rome, in Acapulco, in Antigua; they're shown reading expensive art books, talking Italian to Italians; they get their pictures taken leaving such In-places as La Grenouille, Le Mistral, or one or two other glamor haunts where they go for lunch and eat only a plate of hors d'oeuvres. You see what I mean?"

"Keep coming," I said.

"This fashion world, Mark—it's a symbol of youth, of better education, of wealth, of a special kind of sophistication, of a kind of special know-how. You don't make the list of Ten Best-Dressed Women just by wearing the best clothes. You have to have the right attitudes, involve yourself in the right activities, and own the right possessions."

"You ought to write a book," I said.

"I could—if I could like write," she said. "I was sixteen when I became a model; I was eighteen when Nikos took me out of that and made me his—his—"

"Secretary," I reminded her.

"I'm trying to be honest with you, Mark! I—I was a kind of special kind of model for him, if you see what I mean."

"Not yet."

"The designer he's interested in—it's Max now, but there have been a lot of others before Max—would produce the designs and a few samples of a new collection. Like there'd be a see-through evening gown. 'Try it, Jan,' he'd say to me. So I'd put on the dress and go to his rooms. I didn't just strut around, you understand. It would be sort of like a date; we'd talk, and maybe have dinner or a champagne supper, and all the time he'd be looking—"

"At you through the dress," I said.

"That's from Dullsville," she said. "He always said you could never tell about a dress a model parades on the runway at a showing. How would it be if you wore it 'out' somewhere? So I wore them for him—maybe a whole evening. And then he'd thank me very politely and say, 'Tell them yes,' or 'Tell them no, it doesn't send me.' One time a big French designer did a whole line of sleep things—little short chemise-type nightgowns that came down—well, just far enough, and billowy transparent full-length things. Sexual weaponry, Nikos called them. I wore them all one night for him while he sat propped up in bed. And finally he turned thumbs down on them. 'Makes the woman's intention too obvious,' he said. 'Attack too frontal.' He turned down the complete line."

"But he liked to look at you," I said.

"Why not?" she said. "I have a good body." And before I could agree, warmly, she went on. "There are others who had my job before me—and got a little too old, finally. There's a girl in the next room who had it for years, and when she didn't send Nikos any more, he set her up in business for herself. She's one of the top stylists in the fashion world today—Monica Strong. I'm sure he had plans for me when I got too old."

I didn't tell her about Tim Gallivan's remark that she was now a rich and desirable heiress.

"We're drifting away from the people who had a chance to get at that pill bottle," I said.

"His bedroom was like a twenty-hour-a-day night club," she said. "Close people and people he hardly knew milled in and out."

"Let's start with the close ones."

"Monica's still close to him," she said. "She's dark and—"

"I met her when I came in," I said.

"Then you know," Jan said. "She's got style, and she's made it a profession with Nikos's help. He trusted her judgment about clothes. Taste, if you see what I mean. Fashion today like walks a tightrope between good taste and bad taste. A see-through can be beautiful or just plain sexy and cheap." She was checking people off on her silver-tipped fingers. "There's Tim, of course—Tim Gallivan, Nikos's lawyer and financial expert. Tim is a very smart cookie about money, but you put on the Iron Maiden when he's around if you want to stay alive."

"Iron Maiden?"

She grinned at me. "Your chastity belt—your fighting

spurs, if you see what I mean. The world is Sexville to Timmy."

"He bothered you?"

Her face clouded. "Not up to now. Nikos wouldn't have stood for it. But now, well, it looks like I'd have to dust off my track shoes."

"Who else?"

"Right now there are the Faradays—Mike and Dodo. She was Dorothy Dobson before she married Mike. Mike's got money in the Lazar thing—but very hush-hush. He made his money in asbestos—or something. Dodo's important to the Lazar thing. You need the best models, like Suzie Sands and others, to show the collection. But you have to have real people, too. Dodo is no Jackie Onassis or Babe Paley, but she goes to the right places, and she does the right things, and she owns the right possessions. When Dodo wears a Lazar to the opera or to some brawl given by one of the In-people like a Truman Capote, then Maxie will start to get mentioned in the same breath with Balenciaga, Saint Laurent, Norell, and Galanos. Dodo can help make Maxie run—if you see what I mean."

"And Dodo was in and out of Nikos's bedroom?"

"Everybody was. You asked me who was close to Nikos right now. The Faradays are In. Zach Chambers is In—the model agent. Zaccheus Chambers."

"Is he the old camp in the beads?" I asked. "With the jokes?"

"You're behind the times, Mark," Jan said. "Everybody wears beads. Zach could make Nikos laugh until he had to be sent away so Nikos wouldn't have an attack. Then there's Suzie and her lawyer. In or out of clothes, Suzie is the most beautiful girl in the world, I guess. She fascinated Nikos because she's so completely stupid about everything except making money. Then there's Morrie Stein, the photographer.

Morrie is always somewhere, clicking pictures. You could be —well—making love to someone and think you were locked away in a private world, and suddenly you'll hear the click of Morrie's camera, taking shots of you from all angles."

I took a moment to light a cigarette. "These people were all close to Nikos, you say. Why would any of them want to shift his pills so he would die?"

That little-girl frown creased her forehead. "When you were In with Nikos, you were really on top of the world," she said slowly. "If you wanted to buy something, you bought it, no matter what the figures in your own bank account looked like. You asked and you got. But if Nikos turned on you for some reason and you were suddenly Out, it would be like your feet are in a barrel of cement and you're dropped in the river. I mean it would be like Deadsville. Cross Nikos, betray him in some way, and you were a cooked goose without Christmas to go with it. If any of us who were In thought of lining up with another team—well, Nikos had better be dead before you made the move."

"Who was thinking of lining up with another team?"

She didn't get to answer that. The room was suddenly flooded with the sounds of the next-door brawl—voices, laughter, the percussion beat. Then it was shut off and I found myself looking at a man in a brown silk suit, Italian cut, a coffee-colored turtle neck, brown suede shoes. His hair was brown, with a distinguished sprinkle of gray at the temples, worn longish but beautifully shaped by someone like Jerry, the Madison Avenue hair stylist. He had the gorgeous perpetual tan that comes from sunshine and sun lamps. He acted as if I was the invisible man.

"Sorry to have kept you waiting, Doll," he said. He moved with a combination athletic-ballroom grace, and folded Jan in his arms. His wide lips were parted as he kissed her on the mouth and didn't let her go for a long moment. There was nothing brotherly about it. When he did let go of her, he turned to look at me. I found myself being evaluated by the coldest gray eyes I can ever remember seeing.

"This is Mark Haskell, the Beaumont's PR man," Jan said to the brown man. She sounded breathless.

"Michael Faraday," the brown man said, and held out his hand. I braced myself for a crusher and got it. I knew the kind. He would take pleasure in crippling the unprepared. He turned away from me as though that ended me. "Things are pretty hysterical next door," he said to Jan. "Like it must have been when the *Titanic* was sinking. End of the world. I had to stay with Max and some of the others to convince them it was business as usual. That's how Nikos operated. Every eventuality prepared for in advance. The ship isn't sinking at all. Only the captain died."

A brown hand slipped up inside one of Jan's kimono sleeves. The gray eyes turned my way again, hostile.

"If your business with Jan is finished, I'd appreciate your going back to the party," he said. "We have some rather personal matters to discuss."

"See you around," I said to Jan.

She didn't answer or look at me. She was leaning against Faraday, as if the touch of his brown hand inside her sleeve had turned her on. She looked hypnotized.

I stepped through the door to Nikos's bedroom and into Bedlam. The man on the red drums in the room beyond had gone orgiastic, aided by an electric guitar tuned to a decibel maximum. People had to shout at each other to be heard.

Suzie Sands still held court on the bed, with her Tommy tucked in beside her. But the courtiers were new. Zach Chambers had taken his beads and his Merle Oberon story somewhere else. A dark little man in black skintight slacks and a navy turtle neck was taking pictures with a tiny camera of Suzie and her law student. They seemed accustomed to him. He climbed on the headboard behind them and—click! He lay on his stomach on the floor and aimed up at them—click! He stood on a brocaded chair and aimed down at them—click! And people swirled all around him and the scene. I noticed everyone seemed to be getting pretty damn drunk. The photographer, who must be Jan's Morrie Stein, seemed to be part of the scenery to all of them. Suzie fondled her law student's hand, her velvet thigh pressed against his velvet thigh. Lying together on the bed, they looked as if they were floating downstream on a medieval love barge.

I was trying to explain to myself why I was doing a slow burn over Michael Faraday's appearance in Jan's room. His possessiveness toward her had triggered something in me. I didn't resent being treated like a room service waiter. These people were all old friends and I was an outsider. It was the way she'd responded. Maybe most men react as I did when a man comes on the scene whose maleness seems to glow like a neon sign. The minute Faraday had walked into the room I'd disappeared, evaporated, dissolved as far as Jan was concerned. I had been emasculated in one second's exposure to his particular excitement thing. I found I had the rather insane notion of introducing myself to Dodo Faraday in the next room and turning on my own charm—just to show him.

I looked down at my empty martini glass. I must be bombed, I told myself. I started toward the next room and the bar—and Dodo. I didn't make it.

A tawny blonde, messy-haired, in a tweed suit with a very short pleated skirt bore down on me. She had that clean, healthy, sporty look that suggested she could swim, and ski, and dance all night and still look great. She was about thirty, I thought; a good age for an old man of thirty-five like me.

"Hi, Haskell," she said. "I've been looking all over for you. I'm Rosemary Lewis, if you don't know. Rosey to you."

This was the fashion writer Gallivan had mentioned who was riding the Lazar train to glory.

"I was just heading for the martini faucet," I said. "Join me?"

"After I ask you a private question in a far corner," she said. She slipped her arm through mine and started to steer me toward the bathroom. "Safest place," she said. "Even these people won't barge in on you in the john."

I was in the white tiled bathroom and she had locked the door. She parted the mauve shower curtain and looked into the tub, as if she expected someone might be hiding there. When she turned to me, her sociable, chummy smile was gone.

"What's all this chatter about Nikos being poisoned?" she asked me.

So the word was out that there was something non-kosher about Nikos's death.

"Don't give me that innocent look," Rosey said. "If there's a whispering thing going on in this beehive, Pierre Chambrun knows about it. I know his reputation. I suspect that explains your being here, Haskell, to look at girlish thighs with only a casual interest. I suspect you're male enough to respond a little more openly unless you had something on your mind."

I sat down on the john seat and fumbled for a cigarette. The last person in the world Chambrun would want me to talk to was a lady reporter.

"There's a hole in your head I can see through," Rosey said. "You're a secret agent for Chambrun. You're not supposed to talk to anyone, especially not me. Well, you better talk to me, buster, or I'll spill the rumors I've heard in tomorrow's column and you'll have the whole world of communications down on your backs. Convince me I shouldn't scoop the town on this and maybe I'll play ball." Then she smiled that nice, healthy smile. "And give me a cigarette."

I gave her one and held my lighter for her. She had me over a barrel and she knew it.

"It's a dog-eat-dog world, Haskell," she said. She sat down on the edge of the bathtub, and the pleated skirt hiked up, revealing what were not Twiggy pipestems. "There's a hell of a lot of money going into this Lazar promotion. I am—or was—on the gravy train. Nikos liked me."

"He had good taste," I said.

"Don't butter me, chum," she said. "If Lazar comes off—and with a million bucks behind him, he will, or would have—I had an exclusive beat on the whole fashion field. I was the In-kid. If the rumble that's going on here explodes before the showing day after tomorrow, I'm dead. Lazar's collection will be buried under a sensational murder story. I'll still be a dusty runner-up behind the other rag-trade writers. If the roof's caving in, my one chance to stay ahead is to report it in advance. Tell me why I shouldn't."

"You'll blow it anyway," I said. "Any good reporter would."

"You're right," she said, frowning at the ash on her cigarette. "In my trade the name of the game is 'bitchiness.' Beat the competition no matter how—if you want to eat. But I'm a soft-hearted sucker, Haskell. Nikos was my friend. If someone knocked him off, I want his account squared before anything else."

I believed her, and I made up my mind. "He wasn't poisoned," I said.

"You sound certain."

"I know," I said. "But—that's a technicality." I took a deep drag on my cigarette and I told her about the soda mints. Her eyes widened as she listened, and I was suddenly aware they were an extraordinary bright blue.

"That's wild!" she said.

"In spades," I said.

The blue eyes narrowed. "You've thought about this from top to bottom," she said, "and so has Chambrun. You realize there's something awfully long-range and casual about it. When Nikos had an attack, he would die. But there was no way your pill juggler could guess when it would happen. It happened today at four-thirty in the afternoon. But it might not have happened for a week, or a month, or a year. The last one he had was in Paris about six months ago. I was there."

"Someone who was willing to wait a reasonable length of time—to inherit," I suggested.

"Oh, God," she said, "what a line-up! Do you know how Nikos planned things for the people he cared about?"

"Well in advance—with the thought of dying in mind, according to Gallivan."

"That was Nikos," Rosey said. "Max Lazar stood to make a fortune if this promotion worked. But if something happened to Nikos before the big play was made, there is money—like in six figures—for Max to carry on his own affairs. Tim Gallivan is one of the chief heirs in gratitude for twenty years of loyal service. Jan Morse, the current flesh in Nikos's life, will be rich. Monica Strong, who served him well until she got a little too old, will have a wad to carry on her business. Others, in varying substantial amounts—Suzie Sands, Morrie Stein, Zach Chambers. All taken care of in case something happened."

"The Faradays?"

Rosey laughed. "Mike is so rich they don't need help from anyone," she said.

"What about you, Rosey?"

She put out her cigarette on the edge of the wash basin. "The last thing Nikos ever said to me—early this afternoon—was, 'Don't sweat, Rosey. If anything happens to me before you make it big, you'll still eat for a while.' I suppose he made some sort of arrangement for me—like the others."

"What do you mean when you call Jan 'the current flesh' in Nikos's life?"

A strange little smile moved her wide lips. "Nikos was the king of the girl watchers," she said. "I think it must have begun after his first attack of angina. He stopped being an active sexpot and became a watcher. I think that's why he went into the fashion racket. But he was old-fashioned in his tastes, Haskell. Nakedness didn't appeal to him. He was outraged by the topless waitress. Almost moral about it. But when he wanted to look at a girl wearing something suggestive, he wanted it badly—like a thirsty man needs a drink. So he had someone to put on the clothes that gave him a bang. For ten years it was Monica, and then she lost her thing for him. She began to be a little long in the tooth for excitement. But he didn't just throw her out in the dust heap. He set her up in business. She's good at what she does. She learned while she was with him. Now it's Jan; a sort of idiot child, but exciting to Nikos."

"She guessed about the pills—wrong like you, but she guessed," I said.

"It's all over that room out there, like a forest fire," Rosey said. "They think he was poisoned. No one has guessed how it really was. What is your Chambrun doing about it?"

"The police have been notified, but they're staying out for a bit," I said. "Cops on the scene would have everyone covering up, we thought. I'm supposed to be trying to find out who could have switched the pills."

"There's an army of possibles," Rosey said. Her smile was wry. "I think you'd better 'take me to your leader,' Haskell. If I'm to sit on this story, I think I'd better have some sort of guarantee from your side."

3

CHAMBRUN EATS just two meals a day—a hearty breakfast at a quarter to nine in the morning, served in his office, and, twelve hours later, a dinner designed to satisfy his gourmet palate, with wines from the Beaumont's incomparable cellar. The breakfast he eats alone, with the day's business at his elbow. Dinner is something else again. He dresses for the occasion, in a dinner jacket made for him by Kilgour, French, and Stanbury of London. This is not the swank of the Englishman who dresses for dinner even in the African jungle. Immediately after his dinner Chambrun makes the rounds of the Beaumont's night spots: the Blue Lagoon Room and its night-club entertainment, the Trapeze Bar, the Spartan Bar, the Grand Ballroom where there is inevitably a function. I have described this nightly routine as being like Marshal Dillon checking out Dodge City after dark. The dinner jacket is as much a part of his business uniform as is the television marshal's gun belt.

Chambrun's dinner is not something you interrupt. He often has a guest or two—some important personage staying at the hotel, a friend from some other part of the world, a Hollywood star who hopes to avoid the autograph scramble that will take place if he appears in one of the public rooms. There are a few old cronies around town whom he knows from other times and other worlds. Sometimes the guest will be a nobody like me. Chambrun can be a delightful companion in this one time of the day which he insists must be relaxed and divorced from business. We who know him and his every whim would sooner be shot than interrupt this dinner hour.

That night I felt I had no choice. My watch told me that he would be about halfway through dinner when I arrived at his second floor office with Rosey Lewis in tow.

Unless there is a special reason for her to stay, Miss Ruysdale has gone her own mysterious and private way long before the dinner hour. A French waiter named Jacques serves the great man and stands guard outside the inner office door. The hall door to Miss Ruysdale's office is kept locked so there can be no casual drop-ins. I have the key to that door, but I used it that night for only the second time in my five years at the Beaumont.

Jacques, a dark little man, ageless, with long sideburns, was sitting on a straight-backed chair outside the sanctum. Lifted eyebrows showed his surprise at seeing Rosey.

"Company?" I asked him.

"He is alone tonight, Monsieur Haskell. He expects you."

"Expects me?" I said, startled. He hadn't told me to report back at any special time.

"He told me you would come, monsieur."

I heard Rosey Lewis giggle. "Sees all, knows all," she said. "Did he say he was expecting me?"

"He did not mention you, m'am'selle."

Chambrun's dinner was served on a round table placed under the Chagall on the north wall. The cloth had a lace edge. The silver was exquisitely not the hotel's regular service. There were candles, which flickered gently in the draught from the door as I opened it and led Rosey in.

The Great Man was involved in removing the spine from a brook trout with surgical skill. He looked up at me and nodded.

"Good evening, Miss Lewis," he said. "Please join me. Will you have wine, or perhaps after those block-busting martinis you would prefer something stronger?"

"Coffee when it's available," Rosey said.

"Turkish or American?"

"I once tried to gather the material to do a piece on you, Mr. Chambrun, and about all I was able to gather was that you drink Turkish coffee all day. I'd like to try it."

"You'll regret it," I said.

"Mark's tastes in food and drink are grossly undereducated," Chambrun said. He gestured to Jacques, who had followed us in, and who now headed for the Turkish coffeemaker on the sideboard. Rosey and I sat down on either side of Chambrun at the round table.

"You'll forgive me if I continue to attack this trout while it's still edible. How was it you were able to gather so little material about me, Miss Lewis?"

"You wouldn't see me," Rosey said.

Chambrun's eyes twinkled in their deep pouches. "The curse of having a protective secretary," he said.

"She was right, of course," Rosey said. "I was trying to exploit myself, not you or the hotel."

Chambrun nodded. "We should get along," he said. He looked at me. "Well, Mark?"

"Jacques says you expected me."

He smiled faintly. The trout was deboned and Jacques carried away a side plate with the fish skeleton on it. "You would have to find out something in an hour or so, Mark. The next step would then need discussing."

I gave it to him from top to bottom. He ate unhurriedly while I talked. He looked up at Rosey when I'd finished.

"How did this poison rumor start?" he asked.

"I tried to trace it," Rosey said. "Everybody heard it from somebody else. I hadn't gotten anywhere when I saw Haskell and decided I'd better latch onto him."

Chambrun savored a mouthful of trout. "It could be pure coincidence," he said. "Someone starting something for the excitement of it. The pills didn't work. Maybe they were poison. Chatter-chatter. It grew from the pills didn't work to the pills killed him. Somebody hit on a part-truth without knowing it. It must be giving the murderer fits. No one was expected to dream of such a thing."

Rosey helped herself to one of the flat Egyptian cigarettes from the silver box on the table. I held my lighter for her.

"The thing that puzzles me about it," she said, "is the casualness of it. It could have been months before Nikos had any reason to take the pills. These angina attacks didn't come on schedule, you know. The person who switched the pills was evidently willing to wait an indefinite time for results."

"Long-range capital gain," Chambrun said. He touched his lips with a white linen napkin. "Someone looking to a future security."

"It's so damn cold-blooded!" Rosey said.

"And maybe not so casual," Chambrun said. "I need you out of the way. You have angina. The wrong, but harmless, pills would do the job if you had an attack in time to suit my needs. It would be nice for me if that happened, because it would be almost impossible to pin anything on me. But if it *didn't* happen on schedule—well, then I would have to try Plan Two, whatever that may be." He shrugged. "I need money next month. I have that much time to hope Plan One will work. If it doesn't, then I will have to go to Plan Two."

"It should be fairly simple to narrow the field," I said. "Get Tim Gallivan to produce a copy of Nikos's will. Your killer is one of the heirs."

"It wouldn't surprise me to find there were a hundred people mentioned in Nikos's will," Rosey said. "Including me! And Nikos was constantly changing it—adding new friends, subtracting others who no longer needed his help, or who had displeased him."

"Who had displeased him?" Chambrun asked.

"I couldn't begin to guess," Rosey said. "He was surrounded by court jesters, and leeches, and people who stroked his ego for the profit in it. Oh, there are plenty of people he's walked on in the past. He was a ruthless enemy in the business world. But none of those obvious people have been close enough to him, here at the Beaumont, to get at that pill bottle. That had to be someone close; someone who could take the bottle from the bedside table, empty the nitro pills down the john, replace them with soda mints, and get the bottle back before Nikos missed it. He would miss it very quickly, because his life depended on it. But if someone like Suzie or Jan was modeling one of the new Lazar collection for him, or one of those long-haired rock singers was doing a number for him, or Zach Chambers was in the middle of one of his long shaggy dog stories with a sexy twist—well, Nikos's attention might be held long enough for the bottle to be taken to the john and brought back."

"Or while he slept," Chambrun said.

Rosey's healthy face clouded. "There are only two people

who could get to him while he slept," she said. "Tim Gallivan has a connecting room on one side of his suite. Jan Morse has one on the other."

"With the keys on Nikos's side of the door," I said.

"They were unlocked at night," Rosey said. "For all his apparent calm, Nikos was afraid. If something happened to him, he wanted Tim or Jan to be able to get to him without having to send downstairs for a passkey and the house dick."

"They couldn't hear him if he called for help," I said. "The rooms are soundproofed."

"It was their job to check on him at regular intervals," Rosey said.

"You're really up on the intimate details, Miss Lewis," Chambrun said.

Her bright blue eyes looked at him, unflinching. "I traveled with Nikos last spring—Rome, Paris. When Tim was away on a couple of business trips, I took his place in an adjoining room. Jan and I shared the job of checking on Nikos every hour."

"So the night shift could have played games with the pill bottle without too much difficulty," Chambrun said.

Rosey nodded slowly. "It was always there on the bedside table within reach of his hand."

"What about Gallivan and Miss Morse?" Chambrun asked. "I understand from Gallivan himself they are two who stand to benefit most handsomely from Nikos's death."

"I'm only guessing, but I'd say top of the list," Rosey said. "Nikos was a realist. There had to be a couple of people he could depend on without question. All Jan and Tim had to do if they wanted something was ask for it and they got it. No questions asked. Nikos didn't want them waiting for him to die. He had to trust them, so he gave them no reason to be in a hurry."

"How did Nikos feel about Jan's outside sex life?" I asked. "With someone like Mike Faraday, for instance?"

Rosey gave me a wry smile. "You weren't wasting your time in there, Haskell."

"It's a thing, isn't it?" I said, still feeling unaccountably angry about it.

"It's a thing, according to the grapevine," Rosey said.

"Doesn't Mrs. Faraday object?" Chambrun asked.

"Mike Faraday is so rich it would take a lot for Dodo to make trouble. She's too comfortable the way things are. And," Rosey said, her smile turning hard, "she's free to do what she likes with her life."

"I find the New World rather indigestible," Chambrun said. His eyes were almost hidden behind their hooded lids. "It's been very pleasant talking to you, Miss Lewis, but you haven't come to the point."

"Point?" she said.

"You obviously want something from me in return for not producing headlines for tomorrow morning's papers."

Rosey threw back her head and laughed. "I wouldn't like to be married to you, Chambrun," she said. "I don't like having my mind read, and I don't particularly like this Turkish coffee."

"You want a hot line to the center of things," Chambrun said.

"It seems fair, doesn't it?"

"Since they're all talking about it, the story will surely leak," Chambrun said.

"But not what's being done about it," Rosey said. "Not the truth about the pills. Your only weapon at this point is that you know what really happened. I'll hold it back, because I loved Nikos in my fashion, provided I get it in time for a beat when you're ready to talk."

"It seems little enough to offer you for your silence, which we very much need at the moment, Miss Lewis. It's a deal. But cooperation is a two-way street. You're going to be a part of the fashion circus for the next two days. Can we count on you to eavesdrop and pass along anything that might leave us a little less paralyzed?"

"If I think it will help Nikos even his score," Rosey said.

Chambrun stood up. "My cautious secretary will be told you are to be passed through to me any time you ask, Miss Lewis. You're going back to the nineteenth-floor brawl now?"

"It seems the sensible thing to do."

"Mark, take Miss Lewis upstairs, and then come back here, please."

Rosey and I went down the corridor to the elevators.

"Does he always eat dinner in such lonely grandeur?" she asked as we waited.

"Rarely," I said. "Tonight he was expecting me—it seems."

"How do you stand it—having him one step ahead of you all the time?"

"Mostly it's rather comforting," I said.

The elevator door opened noiselessly.

"You don't have to come up with me, Haskell," Rosey said. "I'm a big girl, you know. Thanks for not being stuffy."

The tawny hair glittered in the light from the car ceiling, and she waved at me as the door closed. I watched the little lighted arrow over the door clicking off the floors toward 19. . . .

When I got back to the office, Jacques had cleared away the dinner service and Chambrun was sitting at his desk, slumped down in his chair, his eyes hidden in their deep pouches.

"You did the right thing, bringing her here, Mark," he said, exhaling a cloud of pale blue smoke, "but I'm damned if I know whether it's doing us much good to keep our small secret if everyone suspects there was something fishy about Nikos's death."

"The killer will think we're looking for evidence of poison, when actually we're looking for something else," I said cheerfully.

"What? What are we looking for, Mark? Five billion soda mint tablets have been sold in New York in the last twenty-four hours. What evidence can we expect to find? No fingerprints—no nothing."

"So we stay very close to these fashion kids for the next two days and hope somebody's foot will slip. They do an awful lot of drinking. Someone might get careless."

"And Christmas might come in July," Chambrun said. "But I don't know anything better to do but watch and listen."

"You want me to go back up to nineteen-A?" I asked.

"I think so. But first take a quick tour of the hotel, Mark. I'm anchored here waiting for someone from the police commissioner's office to try to convince me that the Beaumont should be swarming with cops."

No matter what was shaking the earth under our feet, the Beaumont's guests were never to guess that anything threatened the Swiss-watch perfection of the hotel's routines.

It was a reasonably quiet night in the Beaumont. All vestiges of the fashion show had disappeared from the Blue Lagoon Room, presided over with his usual magnificent calm by Mr. Cardoza. Soft lights, soft music, and gourmet food were its principal attraction. A particularly noisy comedian of the Don Rickles school would shatter the quiet during the two upcoming floor shows.

The Spartan Bar, presided over by Mr. Novotny, was

cathedral-quiet. This is a no-women-admitted room which is really a sort of club for elegant old gentlemen. Two white heads were bent over a chessboard in the far corner.

A charity ball for the benefit of a New Jersey PTA occupied the ballroom. The tickets were fifty dollars a head and the place was crowded, but the fashion kids on the 19th floor would have shuddered at the 1935 styles.

I saved the Trapeze Bar till last because it's my favorite hangout in the hotel. I'd had no dinner, and I decided before I went back to the blast in 19A, I'd better have a Jack Daniels on the rocks and a steak sandwich to blot out the memory of that devastating martini schedule.

The Trapeze Bar is suspended in space, like a birdcage, over the foyer to the Grand Ballroom. The walls of the Trapeze are elaborate Florentine grillwork. An artist of the Calder school has decorated it with mobiles of circus performers working on trapezes. They sway slightly in the draught from a concealed air conditioning system, giving you the impression, on your third drink, that the whole place is swinging gently in space. The maitre d' is Mr. Del Greco, who can tell you the exact boiling point of ten thousand of New York's steady drinkers.

The Trapeze was crowded, the atmosphere gay yet orderly. Mr. Del Greco saw me and did something complex with his eyebrows that was plainly asking me whether I wanted to stand at the crowded bar or have a table. I didn't see any empty tables, but I knew one would appear if I asked. I made motions like a man cutting a steak and eating it. And then someone called out my name.

"Mark!"

It was Jan Morse. She was sitting alone at a corner table, something that looked like a Bloody Mary in front of her. She'd changed out of the jump suit into a raspberry-colored wool thing, very short in the skirt, very scooped out at the neckline. Sexual weaponry, I thought, remembering Nikos's phrase by way of Jan. Some of the highest-priced call girls in New York wander in and out of the Trapeze. She looked like luxury goods, I thought, and realized I was still mad at her.

I didn't mean to do more than wave, but I found my feet taking me over to her table.

"I've been looking all over for you," she said.

Mr. Del Greco was at my elbow. "Will you join Miss Morse, or shall I get you a table, Mr. Haskell?"

"You can get me a—"

"Of course he'll join me," Jan interrupted. "We didn't finish what we were talking about, Mark."

I ordered my Jack Daniels and steak sandwich.

"You were asking me who was thinking of lining up with another team when we were interrupted," Jan said.

"Who was thinking of lining up with another team?"

"I haven't any idea," she said.

"You came looking for me to tell me that?" I sounded angry. In spite of myself I was angry.

Her brown eyes were wide, but fixed very intently on me. "I came looking for you because I knew I'd hurt your feelings. I don't like to hurt someone."

"What makes you think you hurt my feelings?"

She reached out and touched my hand. Her fingers were warm. I felt like a seventeen-year-old adolescent out with his first "fast" woman. There were suddenly butterflies in my stomach. I told myself, "React your age, Bud!"

"You don't have control over everything, even if you'd like to," she said. "Mike Faraday sends me, Mark."

"I noticed you weren't wearing those track shoes you mentioned," I said.

Her body moved inside the raspberry wool, as though she

was in pain. "I can't help myself with Mike. It's like I can't kick it. I want to but I can't."

"Look, Doll," I said, emphasizing his name for her, "I can't help you with your little problem. You said Nikos would have been angry if Tim Gallivan made a pass at you. How did he feel about Faraday?"

The brown eyes were wide, disturbingly honest. "He didn't know about Mike. Do you know, that was the first time Mike ever touched me in public? That moment in my room? It was because he didn't have to be afraid anyone would mention it to Nikos."

"A lot of people do know about it, I hear," I said.

"If anybody told Nikos, he would have asked me and I would have lied to him."

"Because you didn't want to lose a very secure future."

"Because I wouldn't have wanted to hurt him," Jan said.

A waiter brought my Jack Daniels and I took a solid swig of it.

"He used to cry sometimes," Jan said.

"Who used to cry?"

"Nikos. He used to cry because he wasn't a man any more. He used to cry because he couldn't make love to me. Oh, I would have if he'd asked. I really loved him, Mark. I wouldn't have hurt him for anything. I know what it was like for him, feeling he wasn't a man any more. That's why I felt so badly about you."

"Non sequitur," I said.

"I made you feel you weren't a man," she said. "Suddenly everything was turned on for Mike and you might like not have been there. It was an awful thing to do to you."

"I'll live," I said. Everyone said she wasn't terribly bright, but she'd hit the bull's-eye. That was exactly why I'd been burning for the last hour—because she'd put my masculinity in doubt.

"Some people think you have to have love and respect and all like that with sex," she said. "To me it's just something you've got, and you give it because it's all you've got to give. So if you feel like giving something to someone, why, you give the only thing you've got."

"Makes it all very simple," I said. My mouth felt suddenly dry.

"So if it would help you to get over being hurt," she said, the wide brown eyes leveled at me without a suggestion of coquettishness, "and it would give you any pleasure—"

Someone was tugging at my coat sleeve and I tried to shake it off. Stupid waiter, I thought. Something about the steak sandwich at a moment like this.

"Sorry to interrupt," a familiar voice said. It was Jerry Dodd, the Beaumont's security officer. Jerry is a thin, wiry man with a professional smile that does nothing to hide the fact his shrewd eyes aren't ever missing a trick. "Speak to you alone a moment—?"

"I don't admire your timing," I said. I stood up and walked a few steps away from the table with him.

"Boss wants you," Jerry said. "Someone took a dive from the nineteenth floor."

"A dive?"

"They're swabbing down the sidewalk now," Jerry said.

"Who was it?"

"Some newspaper dame," Jerry said. "Name of Rosemary Lewis."

Part Two

1

I REMEMBER the Trapeze started to revolve slowly around me. It was nightmarish. I was acutely aware of the smells of perfume and tobacco and liquor and food. A raspberry blonde stared at me through a kind of fog, puzzled that I was walking away from her in the middle of her best offer. Voices sounded loud and harsh.

I was grateful for Jerry Dodd's firm grip on my arm. My legs felt like rubber hose.

"I just left her—not forty-five minutes ago," I heard myself saying to Jerry in a voice that wasn't mine.

"It only takes seconds to hit the sidewalk from nineteen floors up," Jerry said. It was callous. It was like cold water being thrown in my face. I realized afterward that was exactly what he meant it to be like.

We managed to cross the Trapeze, in and out of tables, and reach the hall outside opposite a bank of elevators. I was aware that people watched us curiously. They must have thought Jerry was helping a drunk out of the place. I wondered why we didn't just climb the one flight of stairs to Chambrun's office.

"He's in her room," Jerry told me.

The elevator took us up, my stomach turning over in the swift ascent. I found myself hanging onto the little handrail in the car. I'd known her for less than an hour, but she'd seemed so alive, so competent, so basically *decent*. "I'm a big girl," she'd said, so sure of herself. I closed my eyes, fighting nausea, as I thought of that fine, healthy body hurtling through space to be smashed into unrecognizable bits on the cement sidewalk.

"Do you have any idea who did it?" I asked Jerry as we walked along the corridor to 1919, her room.

"Who did what?" he asked in his flat, unemotional voice.

"She didn't jump!" I said, facing him.

"Who says?"

"I say!" I said, as certain of that as I was of tomorrow's rising sun.

"Let's see," Jerry said. He rang the doorbell outside 1919.

The door was instantly opened by Joe Cameron, Jerry's top assistant on the security force. Joe is an affable redhead, Brooks Brotherish in clothes, looking more like a young Madison Avenue executive than a special cop. He'd been a modern language major at Columbia and he was valuable at the Beaumont, with all the U.N. people we had and other foreign guests.

Beyond Cameron in the room I saw Chambrun, standing in the center of the rug, chin sunk forward on his chest. The room smelled like woman, the perfume painfully familiar, although I'd known Rosey for less than an hour.

Then I felt myself sucking for breath. On the dressing table just beyond Chambrun was Rosey's tawny blond messy hair. It was on a little round stand, the shape of her head. Cameron must have sensed my reaction.

"Smart women wear wigs half the time," he said. "She had a couple more in the closet—one red, for red-haired fanciers, I imagine."

The room was neat. There were no signs of any hasty clothes-changing; certainly no sign that Rosey had put up any kind of a fight. The two windows were shut tight, and I was aware of the soft purring of the air conditioner fitted into one of them.

I started, trancelike, toward the window. Nineteen stories to the street!

"Don't touch anything," Chambrun said sharply. He looked at me and his face was rock-hard. "You brought her up here?"

I shook my head. "I—I left her at the elevator on your floor," I said. "She said—she said she was a big girl. I—"

"I don't think she ever came here," Chambrun said. "There's no ledge outside the windows on this floor. You can't stand outside the windows and close them."

"She never in God's world jumped!" I said.

"I'm inclined to agree. I don't think anything at all happened in this room. Wherever she went out, it wasn't here."

I turned to Jerry. "You—you had no problem identifying her?" I wanted him to tell me she hadn't been totally destroyed, I think.

"Room key in her handbag," Jerry said.

"Then can you be absolutely sure—?"

"Pull yourself together, Mark," Chambrun said. "It was Miss Lewis."

"She was going back to the party," I said.

Chambrun nodded and turned to Joe Cameron. "You wait

here, Joe, for the homicide people," he said. "You two come with me." He headed briskly for the corridor with Jerry and me at his heels.

Nobody answered our doorbell ring at 19A. Chambrun tried the door and found it on the latch. He opened it and we were blasted by sound. The drummer and guitar player were ear-splitting. Half a dozen people were dancing the frug or what have you in the center, surrounded by a score of others who were stomping and clapping to the rhythm. One of the dancers was Dodo Faraday, in her snowflake decorated brocade. She seemed to have come very much alive. Zach Chambers, the beaded camp agent, was her partner. I saw Max Lazar by the fireplace. I don't think he'd moved since I'd first come to the party. I wondered if he took his elbows off the mantel if he wouldn't fall flat on his face. Standing in the center of a stretcher table against the far wall was Morrie Stein, snapping pictures of the dancers. He must have used eight miles of film since I'd seen him last. The redhaired girl with the stay-put lipstick was bearing down on Chambrun. I had an idea she might be in for a surprise.

And then Monica Strong was with us, intercepting the redhead with an impatient gesture.

"Good evening, Mr. Chambrun," she said in her low, throaty voice. "I'm afraid you'll never catch up with this mob. Can I start you trying? Martini? Scotch?"

"This isn't a social call, Miss Strong," Chambrun said. His narrowed black eyes darted around the room. "Do you know where I can find Timothy Gallivan?"

"By this time I should imagine in his room—with company," she said dryly.

"Would you have someone get him for me?"

She nodded and turned to the red-haired tootsie. "Will you tell Tim he's wanted? Urgent, I imagine."

The redhead giggled. "He won't like my barging in."

"So barge, darling," Monica said. She turned back to Chambrun. "I understood these rooms were soundproofed."

"They are."

"Then you're not here to complain about the noise?"

"I'm not," Chambrun said. "Have you seen Rosemary Lewis anywhere about?"

"Rosey?" Not a thing about the lovely face suggested any concern. "The last I remember was seeing her leave the party with Mr. Haskell," she said.

"Since then?"

"I don't recall. The traffic's pretty heavy here. She could have come back and gone again. I didn't notice. She doesn't seem to be here now. Unless—"

"Unless what, Miss Strong?"

"She might be with Tim," she said.

"It's like that?"

"It's like anyone might be with Tim," she said dryly.

"She's not with Gallivan," Chambrun said. "She's dead."

The gray-green eyes widened. "I don't think I understand."

"She's dead," Chambrun said.

"We scraped her up off the sidewalk," Jerry Dodd said in his cold, flat voice.

A hand went up to Monica's lips. "Oh, my God!" she whispered.

"The last we know about her was that she was headed back up here to the party," Chambrun said. "Half an hour or so later she fell—or something—to the street."

"How perfectly ghastly!"

"We need to know where and how it happened," Jerry said.

"Surely not here," Monica said. "You see how crowded it

is. There'd be no chance—I mean, with all these kooks!"

The two-man musical horror was shouting at the top of its lungs. Monica turned toward them as though she intended to stop all the noise.

"Let things go on," Chambrun said. "I don't want this news spread until the police get here. There'll be questions. We can't have people leaving."

"Why? Why did she do it?" Monica asked. "Things were so right for her just now. All the things she'd wanted for herself—her career—were just around the corner."

I was looking around for Jan's sex king. He didn't seem to be there to watch his wife cavort.

"Both of them on the same day!" Monica said. "Both so alive, so keen about everything."

Chambrun faced her. "Who didn't like Miss Lewis?" he asked.

The gray-green eyes narrowed. "Are you saying she didn't —it wasn't suicide, Mr. Chambrun?"

"It could very well not have been," he said. "I'd swear the thought hadn't crossed her mind half an hour before it happened. I could be wrong. Some people act out a kind of gaiety till the very last moment."

"There's been a lot of crazy talk here all afternoon about Nikos," Monica said. "That he was poisoned. I laughed it off. You know how people are. But my God, could they both—is it possible they were *both*—helped along?"

"It's possible, Miss Strong." He shuddered as the drummer beat out something on his bongos. "Our problem here is to talk to someone who's stayed reasonably sober. You may be elected by default. How do they stand that noise?"

"Each generation to its own thing," Monica said. "My mother was frowned on for doing the Charleston."

I saw Tim Gallivan emerge from the bedroom. He had on

the blue chino slacks and the turtle-neck sweater, but he'd left his brown loafers behind. He was barefoot. He looked a little flushed and annoyed, but when he saw Chambrun, a kind of toothpaste smile moved his Irish face.

"You changed your mind," he said. "I'm afraid the evening has gone by the point when there'd be any sense in trying to introduce you to these fun-lovers."

"It's not a social visit," Chambrun said. "Where can we talk quietly? Your room?"

Gallivan's smile turned mischievous. "I regret to say I can't offer you my personal hospitality at the moment." He put a hand on Chambrun's sleeve. "If it's something important, can't it wait till morning? I'm neither in the mood nor the right shape for seriousness, Dad. To be honest with you, I'm royally stoned."

"You can use my room if it will help," Monica said.

"Oh, goody!" Gallivan said. "I've been trying to get into a whole series of rooms belonging to you, Monica, for the last ten years. At last I'm going to make it!"

"It's nineteen hundred twenty-one," Monica said. "Right next to—to Rosey's."

Gallivan's grin slowly faded. "It is something serious," he said.

"You mind walking down the hall in your bare feet?" Chambrun asked.

Gallivan's grin re-formed as he looked down at his naked toes. "I was caught, you might say, with my shoes off," he said. "Perhaps I'd better get them and, at the same time, make my apologies. There is a little girl who was about to have a brand-new experience who isn't going to thank you for this, Dad. Back in a trivet."

He weaved his way through the dancers and into Nikos's bedroom, where I assumed Suzie and her law student were still holding court.

The drummer seemed to be beating on some raw, exposed nerves of mine.

"What can I do to help?" I heard Monica asking.

"Keep the party going," Chambrun said. "The police will be on the scene at any moment now. Then what happens is up to them."

It was at that moment that the beaded Zach Chambers gave his dancing partner a particularly vigorous twirl and she seemed to lose her balance and I found myself, unexpectedly, holding the famous Dodo Faraday in my arms. She looked up at me, laughing breathlessly, her dark eyes wide and blurred as though she'd just had belladonna drops in them.

"Home safe!" she said.

She clung very tightly to me, warm, her body still moving slightly to the rhythm of the drums, smelling wonderfully like some exotic florist's shop.

"You're cute," she said. "Unfortunately I don't know you." She twisted away from me. Zach Chambers had her by the wrist again and pulled her back into the vortex of the dancers.

"Poor Dodo," Monica said. "There's no longer any reason for Mike to play it safe with his little blond tart—now that Nikos is gone."

Gallivan reappeared. He had put on his loafers and had added a loose-fitting corduroy jacket, with a white scarf knotted casually at his neck. There was a smear of lipstick near the corner of his mouth. The lady in the bedroom had evidently not been wearing that special new product from Lazar House.

Monica produced a room key from her bag and we went down the hall to 1921—Jerry and I following Chambrun and Gallivan.

The room was in a rather pleasant state of disorder. There were a pair of panty-stockings and a bra lying on the bed, along with a flimsy white dressing gown of sorts. The dressing table was loaded with little jars and bottles, some of them left carelessly open.

Gallivan walked over to the bed and picked up the bra. He grinned at us. "Fellow rarely gets a chance to get turned loose in a woman's room. You get to see how much is real and how much is a put-on." He waved the bra at the dressing table. "Monica has reached the age when an awful lot has to be done to her face and hair. You wonder if she's wearing a padded bra. I'm happy to report she is not. They are real." He tossed the bra back on the bed. "Okay, Chambrun, you've dragged me away from the delights of the flesh. It better be good." He looked at Jerry. "I don't think I know you, chum."

"Mr. Dodd, the hotel's security officer," Chambrun said.

"Well, well," Gallivan said, "has someone stolen the crown jewels? Which reminds me we're going to need extra help from you on Lazar Day. Suzie will be wearing a quarter of a million in real diamonds, loaned by Larry Winsted, the jeweler. He'll have his private fuzz on hand to watch over the beads, but the hotel had better have its eyes open, too. If someone snatched them, the publicity would be bad. Well, what's the big mystery, Chambrun?"

"We are confronted," Chambrun said quietly, "with two murders."

Gallivan laughed and sat down on the edge of the bed. He picked up Monica's dressing gown and sniffed it, like a wine fancier. "Anyone I know?" he asked.

"Quite well," Chambrun said. "Nikos and Rosemary Lewis."

Gallivan stared at him, and the dressing gown slipped out

of his fingers to the floor. "What the hell are you talking about?" he said.

What happened was rather extraordinary. The half-potted gent interrupted in the middle of a dalliance, grinning and joking, was turned off like a light switch. The blue eyes, fixed on Chambrun, were cold and calculating. He was suddenly Nikos Karados's lawyer. He listened intently while Chambrun laid it on the line for him—the pills, the terrible plunge to destruction by Rosey.

"If I can put my hands on the sonofabitch who played games with Nikos's pills, you won't need the cops," he said when Chambrun had finished. He took a cigarette out of his pocket and lit it. "You don't know that Rosey didn't jump of her own free will."

"Evidence, no," Chambrun said. "Convictions, yes."

Gallivan took a deep drag on his cigarette. "I'm inclined to agree," he said. "Lazar's success or failure day after tomorrow was to be her success or failure. She had everything going for her right now." He looked up. "There's an old-fashioned word for Rosey. Gallant. She's been in the front-line trenches all her life, bloody but unbowed. And she was about to win the war, for God sake." He shook his head from side to side. "Maybe she had a terminal cancer; maybe she couldn't stand the pain. But knowing her, I'd bet a hundred to one she'd have borne anything until after the verdict was in on Friday. My convictions are the same as yours, Chambrun. She didn't jump."

"We don't know yet where it happened," Chambrun said. "In a few minutes Homicide will be in charge. There are a hundred people down the hall. Every one of them will be questioned. Every room on this floor—in the whole hotel, if necessary—will be searched. I choose to think, at the moment, that after Miss Lewis left my office, in possession of all the facts about Nikos, she hit on the truth about it. Instead of keeping it to herself and bringing it to me, she faced someone with it in her forthright fashion. It cost her her life."

"Possible," Gallivan said, staring at a pattern in the center of the rug.

"So my primary concern, Gallivan, and yours is who wanted Nikos dead and why. Sooner or later we'll find out from which window Miss Lewis was thrown. It may not tell us anything. There's been time for the killer to cover all traces. Privacy is not the name of the game up here on the nineteenth floor. You're all in and out of everybody's rooms. No one is going to remember who was in what room or what bed at any given time. The quickest way for us to get at the core of this is to identify the person who wanted Nikos dead, and you, his closest associate, should be able to provide us with short cuts."

Gallivan didn't answer. He sat, turning his cigarette around in his fingers, staring at the rug pattern.

"You know all about Nikos's private plans and projects," Chambrun said. "You know the contents of his will, as his lawyer. You know who stands to benefit by Nikos's death."

Gallivan lifted his head and his smile was wry. "So let us begin with Timothy Joseph Gallivan," he said. "When the will is probated, I will come into a cool two and a half million dollars in tax-exempt government bonds. How do you like that for a motive? I will also collect executor's fees which won't be hay. I am a director on the boards of a dozen businesses that will continue to operate, and I won't just get a five-dollar gold piece for attending an annual stockholders' meeting. I am at this moment, Chambrun, as a result of Nikos's death, a very rich man with power in a very considerable business empire."

Chambrun's face was a mask. "And were you in a hurry to

come into all this wealth and power, Mr. Gallivan?"

Gallivan laughed. "Would you believe it if I told you that my salary for acting as Nikos's legal adviser and his stand-in in a score of power complexes amounted to about a half million dollars a year—after taxes? I haven't figured it out, but the chances are I've had more spending money while Nikos was alive than I will have now. Less spending money now, but more power." He took a deep drag on his cigarette. "Nikos saw himself as a kind of god," he said. "Aside from substantial gifts to charities—primarily to cancer and heart disease research—he has left money on the basis of what he considered his infallible judgment of people. For example, Jan Morse gets a half million dollars—but in trust. My guess is that she'll have an income of about thirty thousand a year for life. Motive? Well, it will actually be a comedown for our Jan. Yesterday if she wanted to buy a thirty-thousand-dollar diamond shoe buckle, all she had to do was ask and Nikos would buy it for her. Today she's going to have to struggle along on thirty G's a year and no indulgent papa to buy the extra do-dads. Nikos didn't trust her with the principle. You know why? She's a big-hearted slob who would have given it all away to her friends before Nikos was cold in his grave. Monica Strong was something else again. She gets her half million outright, to spend how and when she pleases. He considered Monica sensible. Max Lazar gets a hundred thousand a year for five years, and then good night. Nikos felt if Max wasn't making it on his own by then, he wasn't worth supporting. There are a hundred others who get all the way from five hundred bucks to a hundred thousand outright. I'd have to go to my records to supply you with a list."

"There's a good chance," Jerry Dodd said, speaking for the first time, "that one of the smaller inheritors would be in more of a hurry than people like Mr. Gallivan and Miss Morse, who were doing fine the way things were. The little guy who needs a thousand bucks to pay off his bookmaker is the dangerous kind."

"Funny you should use that image," Gallivan said. "The big horse better in our little world is Zach Chambers. He makes his living producing the most beautiful women in the world to model clothes, and he spends it at racetracks all over the country. I don't think he's ever seen a horse race in his life —just the odds on his bookmaker's blackboard."

"And he's an heir?" Jerry asked.

"A lot of people who come in for something in the will are getting like severance pay. Max Lazar, for example. Five years and out. Nikos felt a lot of these people have given their time and energy and made their business plans on the assumption of his support. They aren't to be cut off like today. Max has five years to get his business in order. Zach Chambers gets fifty grand a year for three years. That represents what he could expect to make in commissions off model services for Nikos's enterprises alone. He won't lose that until he has ample time to turn around." Gallivan laughed. "Do you know who's in the will, Chambrun? That elegant Mr. Cardoza who's the maitre d' in your Blue Lagoon Room, and Mr. Del Greco who has the same job in the Trapeze Bar. Nikos figured he probably went into each of those places ten times a year. Each time he slipped the maitre d' a fifty dollar bill. 'They probably count on it for Christmas,' Nikos told me. Each of them is down for five hundred bucks. The will is full of little items like that. Nikos hasn't forgotten anyone who ever gave him pleasure or first-class service."

"Was anyone he ever knew left out?" Chambrun asked with a kind of impatience.

"You, Chambrun," Gallivan said, grinning. "Oh, he talked about you. He thought of you as one of two or three people in his lifetime whose friendship wasn't based on what they thought they could get out of him. He decided that to leave you money would lead you to think he felt he had to pay you for your friendship."

"Is there anyone in the will who risked being cut out of it for some reason?" Chambrun asked.

Gallivan's Irish face was screwed up into a kind of rueful grin. "We all did," he said. "Some people thought Nikos was a man subject to whims. He wasn't. But he had his own peculiar code, and if any of us violated it, we would get the ax—boom!"

"What kind of code?"

"Taste—morality."

"Morality!" Jerry exploded. He was thinking of the mob in 19A, I imagine, and Gallivan with his shoes off and his lipstick smear.

Gallivan's grin broadened. "Not yours or mine, Dodd. His—very special. Take his attitude toward sex. It was wide-open, free. Have your fun, baby, with anyone any time. But be exhibitionistic about it, and you were dead. If I used what I wanted to excite anybody but the lady involved, I'd be out selling papers on the corner. If I had a thing with another guy's wife, it was okay with Nikos. But if I made a public sap out of the husband—boom! The public picture was important to him, not the private one. Steal and get away with it and it might amuse him; be caught and publicly exposed and you were from Deadsville. His taste in fashion is a point. It took him a while to get used to the near-nudity that's part of the pop thing. He could take the see-through evening gowns the ladies wear today, but not outright nudity. He fired one of the best models Zach ever produced because she allowed herself to be photographed in one of Rudi Gernreich's topless bathing suits for a magazine. People thought she was fired because she'd posed in a rival designer's thing. Not so. Public nudity was out with Nikos. Oh, yes, violate his idea of good taste and common morality and you'd be cut out of his will so fast—"

"Has it happened?"

"A dozen times, I'd guess."

"Any of those people around here today?"

"Look, Chambrun, you'd not only be cut out of Nikos's will, you'd be cut out of his life."

Chambrun made a restless move to the far corner of the room and back. "The thing I can't get to work for me is the fact that the killer, in Nikos's case, wasn't in a hurry. He was prepared to wait for Nikos to have an attack. So he wasn't afraid, at least for the moment, that he would be discovered in violation of Nikos's code—at least not in the near future. He didn't have a bookmaker standing over him with threats of instant violence. He had time."

"Not in the case of Miss Lewis," Jerry Dodd said. "Instant blackout!"

Chambrun nodded. "And if we're right about her, we're faced with an interesting fact. I'd swear when she left my office she had no idea who had meddled with Nikos's medicine. A little more than half an hour later she was violently destroyed. In that time she must have stumbled on the truth, the facts. The killer didn't have time any more. Miss Lewis had caught him out, and he stood to be nailed for a murder. She was on the inside; she evidently developed a quick hunch. It would seem she solved the case in half an hour's time."

"Which means the answer is lying right around here for us to find," Jerry said.

"Except that we're not on the inside as she was," Chambrun said. His bright black eyes were focused on Gallivan. "Unless you're prepared to really help us, Gallivan. The time for scuttlebutt is over."

"Sure I'll help," Gallivan said. "I want to help." He rubbed a hand over his eyes. "But I—I'm still a little bit in shock, Chambrun. I don't know where to begin." . . .

My own state of shock had drifted away and left me in a state of slow, burning anger. If I told you that part of that anger was based on the fact that the Beaumont was about to be exposed under the glare of a scandalous spotlight, you'd think it didn't make sense. The Beaumont is my life. Its reputation is as important to me as—as my mother's! But that really wasn't at the core of it. We are living in a time when a kind of senseless violence, man against man, is the theme song of the day. You read about it in the papers and you see it on television and you are intellectually outraged by it, but it doesn't happen to you. Then, one day, it does happen to you, and a lot of banked fires in you begin to burn red-hot.

Somewhere, probably within calling distance down the hall, was a man—or a woman—who had calmly planned to kill Nikos Karados for private reasons of gain, and when caught out had instantly struck at Rosey Lewis, who was a decent, straight-shooting gal trying to get at the truth about a monstrous piece of anarchy. I hardly knew Rosey at all, and yet she was me, and Chambrun, and everyone else who believes in an ordered, safe world. Rosey had discovered the truth and paid for it with her life. But I could have stumbled on that same truth and gone out that same window, just as instantly and unhesitatingly as she had.

Our conversation with Gallivan came to an end when Joe Cameron stuck his head in the door and told us that Lieutenant Hardy and the boys from Homicide had arrived. Hardy is an old friend. He has been involved with us at the Beaumont on several occasions. He is a stocky blond who looks more like a Notre Dame fullback than a cop. His technique is a kind of dogged thoroughness.

We all went out into the corridor together and Gallivan headed back for the brawl in 19A with instructions not to start a panic. Jerry Dodd and Joe Cameron went next door to Rosey's room, but Chambrun held back, checking me.

"What's happened to your girl friend?" he asked me.

"What girl friend?"

"Miss Morse."

"I was with her in the Trapeze when Jerry brought me the news. I don't know where she is now."

"Find her and stick with her," Chambrun said.

"Why, for God sake? She—"

"She was the first one to guess that something was wrong with Nikos's medicine," he said. "She's on the inside. She might guess at the truth just as unexpectedly as Miss Lewis did. Till Hardy gets organized, we shouldn't let her run risks."

He was right, of course. We were up against someone who didn't hesitate to counterpunch.

"She may be back at the party by now," I said.

"Stay with her," Chambrun said, "and watch your step."

I went back down the hall toward 19A, but when I came to the door of Jan's room, I rang the bell. No answer. So I went on to 19A again.

The party was still rolling. Nobody seemed to have left. Max Lazar was still propped up at the mantel. The dancing had stopped, but it seemed it was only an opportunity for the dancers to refill their drinks at the bar. Zach Chambers was telling a joke that resulted in hysterical laughter from the little group around him. The tireless musicians were still at it.

There was no sign of Jan.

I thought I'd try her room from the connecting door in

Nikos's bedroom.

The bedroom had quieted. Suzie and her law student were still stretched out on the bed, but the young man appeared to have passed out or gone to sleep. There was a lot of traffic back and forth from the john.

I went over to the connecting door to Jan's room. The key was missing from the door. I didn't know whether to be concerned for Jan or to be annoyed at the possibility that she'd found somebody more attractive than me to give the only thing she had to give. I knocked on the door, hard and insistent.

"You won't be appreciated," a slurred voice said behind me. "Locked doors are locked doors."

I turned and found Dodo Faraday looking up at me. The fumes of perfume and gin were mingled as she came very close and put her hands up on my shoulders.

"I still don't know who you are," she said, "but you're still cute. Maybe I don't care any more that you're a stranger."

She kissed me on the mouth, standing on tiptoe to reach me. I put my hands on her arms to push her away. Her skin was cold and clammy. I thought she must be just on the verge of passing out.

"They're in there?" I asked.

"Who, cutie-pie?"

"Your husband and Jan?"

"Who knows who's with Jan?" she said.

"I don't want to be crude," I said, "but I've got to talk to Jan, whoever she's with."

One of the cold hands touched my cheek. "There are other fish in the sea, cutie-pie," she said.

I turned away and hammered on the door with my fist.

"There are some people who will stop to answer the phone in the middle of love-making," Dodo said, "and I suppose there are others who will get up to answer a knock at the door. But our Jan isn't either kind. Let's go have a drink and decide how to wind up the party."

At which moment the door opened and was filled by the square-shouldered bulk of Lieutenant Hardy.

"Oh, it's you, Haskell," he said. "Come in if you want. This is where she went from."

"What do you mean—where she went from?"

"The Lewis woman," Hardy said. "She went out the window in here." . . .

The room was filled with people. Chambrun and Jerry Dodd and Joe Cameron were there, along with two of Hardy's men, who were at the window, working with tiny vacuum cleaners and a camera. Crouched on a chair in the far corner of the room, looking as though she was trying to press back through the wall, like a cornered animal, was Jan. She saw me come into the room and she looked at me as though I was a stranger she'd never laid eyes on before in her life.

Joe Cameron was closest to me and I looked my question at him. "Window open," he said. "Piece of tweed cloth from the Lewis woman's suit caught on the corner of the air conditioner. The Morse girl called us seconds after you left us to go back to the party. She was trying to reach you, and the switchboard understood you were with us in Miss Strong's room. We took the call. Not much doubt."

"Of what?"

"This is where the Lewis woman took her dive," Joe said. "The ripped piece from her clothes; this window is pretty directly above the spot where she hit the pavement."

"Can I talk to Jan?"

Joe shrugged. "Unless Hardy stops you. He hasn't got to her yet."

This room was painfully quiet in contrast to the party. The two technicians at the window talked to each other in low monotones that I couldn't hear. Chambrun was giving Hardy a rundown on the whole story. They were like people talking in church.

I went over toward Jan. She tried to pull back from me, but the wall wouldn't let her. The brown eyes, wide, dilated, were flooded with terror.

I squatted down beside the chair. "I'm sorry I wasn't here," I said. "Actually I was looking for you."

She looked at me as though the words didn't mean anything.

"I heard about Rosey in the bar downstairs," she said in a dull voice, as though it was something she'd learned by rote. "I came up to my room. The window was open, and I never had the window open because of the air conditioner. I went to close it and saw that piece of cloth flapping in the breeze. I recognized it. I called for help."

"Who told you about Rosey?"

"I—I overheard your conversation with the house detective."

It was possible. Jerry and I had only moved a few feet away. My own state of shock at the time made it difficult to remember whether we talked loudly, or how we talked.

"I was looking for you because you may be in trouble," I said.

"*May* be?"

I looked back over my shoulder and saw that Hardy and Chambrun were both watching us. The official boom was about to be lowered.

"You can trust Lieutenant Hardy. He's a good cop, a good guy," I said. "You can trust everyone in this room, Jan. But no one else. You understand? We think Rosey was killed because somehow she came on the truth about Nikos. You guessed he was deliberately killed. If you've come up with any notions about who or why, don't mention it to anyone except the people here. No one, you understand? Not even your boy friend. If anyone dreams you're on the track, the same thing could happen to you that happened to Rosey."

She reached out and cold fingertips touched my hand. "Mark, I'm so scared! So damn scared!"

"You should be," I said. "Don't trust anyone except the people in this room, you understand?"

She nodded. Her fingers tightened on my hand and she looked past me to Hardy and Chambrun, who were coming her way. "Oh, God!" she whispered.

I stood up beside her, my hand on her shoulder. I could feel her whole body trembling.

Hardy can be a very tough cookie. I've seen him work on a suspect who wouldn't play ball. He can also play it with sympathy.

"At the moment I just want facts from you, Miss Morse," he said. "Evidence seems to indicate that Rosemary Lewis either jumped or was thrown from that window. This is your room. You made the discovery. Will you be good enough to tell me exactly how it came about."

I gave her an encouraging little pat.

"There's a party next door, as you know," Jan said, her voice unsteady. "I—I didn't go to it. I know Mr. Karados wanted everyone to be gay, but I couldn't get myself into the mood, somehow. I was in here when Mr. Haskell came in through the door from Nikos's—Mr. Karados's—bedroom. Then another friend of mine came in while Mark was here and I—well, I was rather rude to Mark."

"Go on, Miss Morse."

"Well, when my other friend left me, I went looking for

Mark. I wanted to—to apologize for having been—rude to him. I—I found him eventually in the Trapeze Bar and we sat down at a table together. Then the house detective came—that man over there—and took Mark a few steps away from the table. I could hear what he said, though. That Rosey had—had killed herself—or been killed. I guess Mark was as stunned as I was. He didn't come back to the table or explain anything. I sat there for a few minutes—like I couldn't move. My legs wouldn't work. Finally I—I came back up here—into this room. I—"

"You came in from the hall, not through the suite next door?"

"Yes."

"Letting yourself in with a key?"

"Yes."

"Then the door from the outside hall was locked?"

"Oh, yes. I always keep it locked. Like some complete stranger could just stroll in."

"So you came in here—"

Jan nodded. "As soon as I switched on the lights, I saw something was wrong. I mean, the window was open—raised up above the air conditioner. I—I never opened the window, because the air conditioner made things fresher, like less pollution, if you see what I mean. So I went over to close it, and just as I started to pull it down, I saw—" She lowered her eyes. "I saw the piece of cloth from Rosey's suit. I recognized it because it was a piece of tweed Nikos had bought in Ireland and given to her. From what I'd heard downstairs, I knew—I thought it must have happened to Rosey like in here. So I tried to call Mark on the phone and I was connected with you, Lieutenant."

Hardy's face wore its sympathetic mask. "Now about the other door into the suite, Miss Morse. It was locked just now when Haskell knocked. The key was on this side. Had it been that way all evening?"

"Oh, no," Jan said. "Normally it wasn't ever locked. Mr. Karados—well, he liked to be able to come and go. I never thought of locking it."

I saw Hardy's face muscles tighten. "But it was locked just now."

"Oh, yes. I locked it," Jan said. "Like I didn't want people barging in and out after I found what I found and called you, Lieutenant."

"Before that it was unlocked?"

"Oh, yes. Mark will tell it was unlocked when he came to see me earlier in the evening. It was never locked."

"Even when you left here and went looking for Haskell in the Trapeze?"

"I never thought of locking that door."

"Then Miss Lewis could have come from the party into this room without any problems?"

"Anyone could," Jan said. "I mean like the door wasn't locked."

"But would Miss Lewis have come in without a 'May I?' or a 'please'?"

"Of course. Rosey and I were really good friends. If she wanted to freshen up, or like go to the john with a little more privacy than she could get in there; or if—if she wanted to talk to someone away from all that noise—"

"She wouldn't have hesitated to use this room?"

"Of course not. I mean, why should she?"

"She didn't ask you if she could use your room to talk to so-and-so?"

"But no! I—I hadn't seen her since before Nikos died in the Blue Lagoon."

"So any of those drunks in the next room could come in

here without any problem. Weren't you afraid someone might take something—jewelry, for example? I notice a case there on the bureau full of things that aren't glass beads."

"The people at the party were my friends," she said, as though that explained everything. "The jewelry—like they were all gifts from Nikos. Even if some of my friends are a little light-fingered, they wouldn't take anything Nikos had given me. He would have been annoyed, and that could be dangerous."

Hardy looked at her as if she was slightly off her rocker. "But nobody *asked* to use your room for any reason at all?"

"I keep telling you, Lieutenant, they didn't have to ask. They could just like come in."

Chambrun gave Hardy a wry smile. "Being over twenty-five, Hardy, you're probably not aware that in the new world everyone loves everyone. What's mine is yours."

Hardy shook his head. "One thing seems fairly certain. Miss Lewis came in here from the suite. And whoever came with her or joined her here also came that way. Someone must have seen."

"There's been someone propped up on the bed in there for hours," I said. "Suzie Sands and her boy friend."

Jan giggled, and for the first time she sounded like herself. "Don't count on Suzie and Tommy to have seen anything," she said. "Their eyes are like mirrors that only reflect one thing—like each other. That's all they ever see is each other, and how beautiful they are. When anyone mentions the Beautiful People, Suzie and Tommy think they're being talked about. They don't see or think about anything but themselves."

"Perhaps," Hardy said, "we can prod them into a little reality. I'm sorry, Miss Morse, but I'm going to have to ask you to wait somewhere else. My men are going to have to go over this room and everything in it—top to bottom."

"I don't want to go to the party!" Jan said.

"The party is about to be over," Hardy said, his mouth tightening.

"You can take Miss Morse to my office," Chambrun said. "And stay with her. You understand, Mark? She's not to be left alone."

I understood.

We walked down the corridor to the elevators, her arm tucked under mine, her sharp silver-tinted fingernails biting into my skin right through the jacket. Her long-legged stride matched mine. We didn't talk because there were other people waiting for the elevator. Two elderly gents eyed Jan with a hungry gleam in their eyes.

We got out at the second floor and went to Chambrun's office. I started to use my key to get in and found the door wasn't locked. Inside Miss Ruysdale was at her desk. She had been sent for by the Great Man to help hold the fort. He had evidently phoned her from upstairs, because she was expecting us. She gave me her Mona Lisa smile.

"The main office is yours," she said. "There's coffee on the sideboard and liquor in it. If either of you would like something to eat, there are sandwich makings in the kitchenette."

I remembered I'd never gotten to my steak sandwich in the Trapeze. I hadn't had anything since lunch, and it was now a few minutes past ten.

"Mark seems to have forgotten his manners, Miss Morse," the perfect secretary said. "I'm Miss Ruysdale. If there's anything I can do for you, or get you—?"

"I think I would like just a teeny-weeny drink," Jan said.

"Mark will take care of that for you. I was to tell you that it may be a long wait."

The lighting in Chambrun's office was warm and soft. I went over to the sideboard and made Jan a Scotch, her choice, and a Jack Daniels on the rocks for myself. Jan sat in one of the high-backed Florentine chairs, her long legs stretched out in front of her. In this room with its dark paneling, its deep, rich colors, its feeling of luxury, she reminded me, somehow, of a Matisse painting—the raspberry dress that clung to her lush figure, the soft gold of her hair, the honey shade of her skin, the wide brown eyes looking far away at something mysterious. I could feel a little pulse start to beat in my throat. Oh, I knew what I was refusing to think about. "You're an old man of thirty-five," I told myself. "You're a bodyguard for a girl who might get herself killed. That's all you are, chum."

I took her the Scotch. As she closed her fingers around the cold glass, her eyes contracted and she looked directly at me.

"You hated me for what I suggested in the Trapeze Bar, didn't you?" she said.

I told myself I would now play this like an adult and not a hungry adolescent. "Of course I didn't hate you," I said. "I wasn't exactly flattered by your offer. It was a form of apology, wasn't it? You didn't make me feel irresistible."

She sipped her Scotch, watching me. She was making some kind of assessment in her own terms. "You have a girl somewhere," she said.

"My dear child, I'm thirty-five years old. If I didn't have a girl by this stage of the game, I'd be spending my spare time on a headshrinker's couch."

"I mean an important girl," Jan said. "Have I seen her around?"

"She's in Europe."

"Oh," she said, and took another sip of her Scotch. "What's she like?"

"Shelda? She's not unlike you in coloring, except her eyes are blue. She's, I'd guess, five years older than you are. She's my secretary here at the hotel. It's no secret that we've been living together for two years, and that we'll probably get married within the next two weeks."

I hoped my carelessness about it sounded sophisticated. I knew I was putting it out on the line as a kind of self-protective armor. In spite of it, the pulse in my throat was beating a little faster.

"I never had any lasting relationship," Jan said, looking into the mysterious distance again. "Except with Nikos—and that didn't involve sex. Not like in the usual way." She laughed softly. "I used to think of myself like a chicken on a rotisserie being watched by a hungry man who couldn't eat me because he had an ulcer. I know just being around Nikos had sexual implications, but he was such a darling about it. He was never a lecherous old goat, pawing and touching and leering at me. He loved my being young because it reminded him of when he was young. Having me there helped him keep his dreams of the past alive."

"Of course you had your extracurricular activities," I said, meaning to hurt.

She turned her head to look at me. "I'm sorry you want me so much," she said. "I mean I'm sorry there are things that stand in the way. I guess I have a kind of upside-down idea about sex."

"I'd love to hear what it is," I said, feeling angry at her again.

"The only thing there is between a man and a woman is sex," she said. "They talk about books, and plays, and politics, and whatever, but all the time it's a sex game. I'm not very bright, and I don't really have like any small talk at all. So all the talk, and the dates, and the dinners and the drinks are just put-offs. I mean why go through all that before you come to the point? Because you will come to the point. So—so I come to the point. I knew what you wanted from me the first time you looked at me. Only things got in the way, like Nikos had his attack, and then I guessed about the pills, and then there was Mike—just at the wrong time. And then Rosey—"

"But between rounds you managed to come to the point," I said.

"I don't understand you," she said. "Why are you outraged because an attractive girl says she's willing to give you what you want?"

"I'm not outraged," I said, feeling outraged.

She gave me a long, steady look. "The only other thing I can talk intelligently about is fashion—clothes. We can talk about high fashion, if you want, even if we're thinking about sex."

I drew a deep breath and my mouth felt dry and that damn pulse was still beating in my throat. I walked away from her. "All right, let's talk about fashion," I said. "I don't know anything about the person who's in the center of this madhouse—Lazar. You're all here because of him. You moved in to the Beaumont like an army—you, Nikos and all his satellites. Two people have been murdered and you'll probably go right on, beating your drums, and laughing, and dancing. Lazar is what charges your batteries. What about him? All I've seen is a campy young man, propping himself up on the mantelpiece so that he won't fall down from an overdose of martinis."

Jan laughed, as if she was enjoying herself. I was proving her point, of course. We would not talk about fashion and Max Lazar and we would continue to think about sex.

"Don't sell Maxie short," she said. "You are the Wall Street–Madison Avenue kind of man, Mark. You are very male, and you wear nice conservative clothes, all gray, and brown, and blue. You are thirty-five. More than half the world is younger than you, Mark. So the young men let their hair grow long and turn peacock. That's today, Mark. Nikos understood, and he was really old."

"Good for Nikos," I said, feeling nasty. "He understood everything except that somebody was planning to kill him."

"Poor Nikos," she said.

"Lazar was his boy," I said.

"You are angry because Maxie is different from you," Jan said. "You're angry because I'm different from your girl in Europe. Do I have to like educate you, Mark?"

She wasn't as dumb as she pretended. "Go ahead, educate me," I said.

"Just because Maxie wears tight pants, and beads, and no socks on his feet doesn't mean he's a homo. He's camp, not homo. You use both words to mean the same thing. Camp is taste; homosexuality is a sexual problem. Camp is against being serious; it likes being eccentric especially if it's vulgar and banal; it likes old styles that are funny now, like feather boas and beaded dresses, and old movies. Batman in his Batman outfit is camp; Batman as the millionaire philanthropist is square—is you, Mark."

"Thanks for everything," I said.

"A lot of homosexuals are camps, but not all camps are homos. Maxie is camp, not homo." She smiled faintly. "He's all man, and don't you forget it."

So little Jan had "come to the point" with Maxie, I thought.

"You don't just drape materials on a dressmaker's dummy to come up with fashion," Jan said. "A designer like Maxie has to understand today's woman. He has to be a historian, and an economist, and a sociologist, and a psychologist. He doesn't come up with what he wants; he comes up with what women want. Oh, they don't know what they want till he comes up with it, but if he was wrong, they'd leave him and his ship to sink. Only Maxie is never wrong, because he's all the things I said he had to be, plus he's a man and he knows what women's clothes have to do with what we're not supposed to talk about."

"Sex."

"Yes, Mark."

"Go on about this superior male."

"Maxie comes up with a design and says 'this is it.' But then there has to be money to manufacture and promote; that's where Nikos comes in. Then the clothes have to be properly shown. That's where Monica Strong comes in. You watch on Friday. The clothes will come out, worn by Suzie Sands, and a girl who looks like Julie Christie, and a girl who looks like Audrey Hepburn, full of life and health and joy, and everyone in the room will begin to feel better, and their hearts will beat faster, and they'll already feel ashamed at the idea of walking out on the street in anything but a Max Lazar creation. Monica knows how to stage it, and Suzie and the other girls know how to sell it. But if Maxie wasn't right, if he wasn't exactly Today, the show would flop."

"And is he Today?"

"For certain," Jan said. "Would Nikos invest a half million dollars in him if he wasn't?"

I looked at my glass. It was empty. I looked at Jan. We were going to have to find something else to talk about, and fast.

I went over to the sideboard and poured myself another Jack Daniels. I looked at her glass and saw it was still three quarters full. I took two steps toward her. It was very mathematical. I mustn't go too close.

"I've heard a lot from Tim Gallivan and Rosey and you about Nikos's private dislike for vulgarity," I said. "You say camp likes vulgarity. Did Nikos and Lazar clash? Did Nikos censor his designs?"

Jan laughed. "You don't know Maxie," she said. "He'd throw a million dollars in the wastebasket before he'd let anyone tell him how to create."

"But if Nikos was riding him, maybe he'd figure he could put up with it for awhile if he knew it was going to end; if he knew that the next time Nikos had an attack it would be all over. Then, no more censorship and another half a million dollars to go on with his business. According to Gallivan, that's what's in Nikos's will for your Maxie."

Jan stared at me steadily.

"The same idea occurred to Rosey," I said. "She went back to the party and she told your Maxie that she wanted to talk to him, and they went to your room. Then she laid it on the line for him. Maybe she remembered something, like a time she saw him fooling with the pill bottle. And so your all-male Maxie heaved her out the window, and came back to his mantelpiece and his martini, and his admiring Scarsdale housewives."

Jan continued to stare at me, her eyes widening.

"Your Maxie would throw a million dollars in the wastebasket if anyone interfered with him, you said. So what about a couple of lives? Would he hesitate?"

She still didn't speak. And then I did something I didn't mean to do, not then, not ever. I went over to her chair, took both her hands in mine and pulled her up onto her feet. I pulled her hard against me and I kissed her. It was long, and sweet, and non-acrobatic. I felt as though I was drowning and enjoying it.

I was aware of a loud voice out in Miss Ruysdale's office. The hell with it. Miss Ruysdale could take care of any situation I could imagine. I wanted to whisper things to this astonishing girl, but I didn't want to go away from her warm, soft mouth.

And then the office door burst open and I had to disengage, reluctantly.

Standing there, face as white as chalk, wearing his chocolate-brown ensemble, was Michael Faraday. His eyes were red with rage. His lithe, graceful, powerful body was balanced on the balls of his feet. And then he came at us, jet-propelled. It was so fast I was only just able to push Jan away toward her chair.

He never spoke a word. He just came at me, swinging both murderous fists. I remember raising my hands in an absurd attempt to ward off that first punch. It smashed through my guard as though it was a paper doily. I caught it flush on the chin, and I had no legs. I sat down on the Oriental rug, hard. I heard Jan scream.

I said something meaningless like, "Now, wait a minute!"

I was on my feet because he pulled me up. I tried to clinch, looking over at his shoulder. Miss Ruysdale must be getting help. I hoped she wouldn't stop for a short beer, because I knew, instinctively, that Faraday was going to kill me. He had blown his stack so far that nothing would stop him. I kicked at his shins, but they might have been encased in armor for all the good it did. I tasted blood that was filling my mouth, and he was out of the clinch and beating me down to the floor like a man armed with iron maces. I think I screamed, because I was completely helpless in the path of a murder machine. Roman candles went off in front of my eyes; I felt an agonizing succession of blows at my ribs and stomach.

And then, mercifully, the lights went out.

2

I SMELLED drugstore smells, antiseptic smells. Someone was touching my cheekbone with something, gently, but there was the stinging pain of something put on a cut.

"I think he's coming around," I heard Doc Partridge say. You'd know his voice anywhere. He always sounds angry with the patient, as though he had no right to be hurt or sick.

I tried moving, and it was unpleasant. It was all coming back. I saw Faraday's murderous red eyes bearing down on me. I tried opening my own eyes, but only one of them seemed to work. The room came into a kind of blurred focus.

I was stretched out on the daybed in Chambrun's dressing room, just off the office. I saw Chambrun, his face looking as if it was carved out of stone, with Jerry Dodd just behind him. I tried to grin. My lips felt thick and swollen.

"Thanks for getting here," I said.

Doc Partridge, who had been bent close to me, straightened

up. "Nothing too serious—unless there are internal injuries," he said. "Bruises, cuts—maybe a slight concussion."

"What happened, Mark?" Chambrun asked in a cold, hard voice.

"It—it was all so quick," I said. "Miss Ruysdale can tell you better than I can," I said. "He came barging in here and it was all so quick—"

"Ruysdale can't tell us anything," Chambrun interrupted. "She's in the ICU at the hospital with a possible fractured skull. I found her—and you. We have no idea what happened."

He never called her "Miss" Ruysdale—just "Ruysdale," and yet I knew she was closer to him than anyone on the staff. There were rumors in the back pantries that if there was a woman in Chambrun's life, it was Ruysdale. Don't get me wrong. I know he was concerned about me, but Ruysdale was much more intimately close.

"Let's have it quickly, Mark, without frills," Jerry Dodd said.

"I was in here with Jan Morse. We were—having a drink." No reason to tell them any more than that. Faraday hadn't exploded when he saw me kissing Jan. He'd been under a full head of steam long before that. "I heard someone shouting at Miss Ruysdale in the outer office, and then the door burst open and Faraday came charging in. He never even said a word. He just ran at me like a runaway tank. I never really had a chance to get my hands up before he was destroying me."

The minute I mentioned Faraday's name, Jerry was gone, without waiting to hear the rest.

"What about Miss Morse?" Chambrun asked.

"She's gone?"

"There was no one here but Ruysdale and you."

"I was out like a light almost before I knew what was happening," I said.

"Looks like he was stomped on after he was down," the old doctor said. "We better have X-rays of your insides, Mark."

"Nonsense," I said. "I feel great."

I tried sitting up, and every inch of me hurt. But I made it. I remember fumbling in my pocket for a cigarette. It seemed the nonchalant thing to do. Chambrun took a step toward me and flicked on his lighter.

"I'd appreciate it if you could go to the hospital, Doctor," he said. "I'd feel better if I knew I wasn't getting any double-talk about Ruysdale's condition."

"Sure, Pierre, I'll go at once," Partridge said. He glared at me. "You ought to come along with me."

"I'll ride it out till morning, Doc," I said. "It doesn't feel like anything's broken. Just a little bent. Mr. Chambrun may need me."

"Your funeral," Partridge said, and stalked away.

"You think you can make it into the next room?" Chambrun asked when we were alone.

"Why not? I'm really fine," I said.

I stood up, and the room started to revolve. I thought my knees were going to buckle and I hung onto the back of a chair. I stood there for a moment, with Chambrun watching me closely, and then the room leveled off and stayed put. I followed him, gingerly, into the office. One of the big Florentine chairs was overturned. Aside from that there was no sign of the fight. Chambrun went over to the sideboard and made me a Jack Daniels on the rocks and poured himself a cup of Turkish coffee. He brought the drink and his coffee back to the desk and sat down in his deep armchair. His eyes were little black slits in their pouches.

"What the hell were you doing with Miss Morse?" he

asked in an unfriendly voice.

For him, the truth. "I was kissing her when he smashed in here," I said. "But that isn't what set him off. I heard him yelling at Miss Ruysdale before he ever came in here."

"That bastard!" Chambrun said, his voice suddenly unsteady with anger. "Her jaw is broken, Mark. He evidently knocked her over backwards and she struck her head on the corner of the desk. So help me God—" He let it ride there, his face working.

"It was like something you wouldn't believe," I said. "The door nearly came off its hinges when he smashed his way in. He never stopped moving. Just came right at me."

"What do you know about him and the Morse girl?"

"They're a thing," I said. "How did he know she was here?"

"It was no secret," Chambrun said. "He might have asked one of Hardy's men. We didn't make a public point of the fact that she might be in danger. You brought her down here while the cops were going over her room. Was it enough of a 'thing' for him to go berserk when he heard she was alone with another man?"

"Something set him off in a big way," I said.

The house phone rang on Chambrun's desk and he picked it up and answered. He listened, frowning, and then said, "Thanks, Jerry." He replaced the receiver.

"Faraday left the hotel with the Morse girl half an hour ago. Mike Maggio and Waters both saw them go."

Maggio is the night bell captain, and Waters is the doorman.

"The last time I was at the party in nineteen-A, Mrs. Faraday was there," I said. "She's obviously not unaware. She might know where he hides out with his extra women."

"Can you make it?" Chambrun asked.

"Sure," I said. The Jack Daniels seemed to have worked a small miracle on my tender insides.

Chambrun stood up. "When I come face to face with that sonofabitch, he's going to discover there are ways to be crushed that don't involve muscle!"

The party was dead, a corpse. Hardy's men had put a blight on it with the word about Rosey Lewis. The red drums and the steel guitar were on chairs in the corner, but no musicians. The green walls with their Flemish paintings looked mournful. The Scarsdale housewives had evaporated. I learned later that all the names and addresses had been carefully noted, that no one was supposed to leave the hotel, but that they'd been given permission to go somewhere for food—which I suspected everyone needed to combat martini anesthesia.

There were still two people in the room, standing over by the bar. I had been wrong about Max Lazar. He could still navigate and he was making himself a fresh martini on the rocks. Monica Strong was with him. Monica's eyes widened when she saw me.

"What on earth happened to you?" she asked.

I hadn't taken time to look at myself in the mirror. I discovered later I looked like Kirk Douglas after his last beating in *The Champion*— swollen eye, cut cheekbone, thick lip.

"I got mixed up with a stone-crusher," I said. "We're looking for Dodo Faraday."

"Oh," Monica said, as though that explained everything. "She was here. She may have joined some of the others in a search for something more nourishing than caviar." Her eyes narrowed. "Did Mike do that to you?"

"Mike—and six other guys, naturally," I said.

"You should learn to stay away from rabbit women,"

Monica said. She turned to Chambrun. "There seems to be some sort of conspiracy against our getting our show on the road, Mr. Chambrun. How much more can happen?"

He looked at her as though he didn't quite believe what he'd heard.

Max Lazar had joined us. He held a glass in one hand, and with the other he stroked the rich fur of his cowboy vest. I thought he must be very drunk, but he was quite steady on his pins.

"I haven't had the pleasure of meeting you, Mr. Chambrun," he said. It was Oxford English with a slight accent which I took to be French. He spoke carefully, as if to make certain he didn't slur the words. "This is all a disaster beyond belief. Poor Rosey. She was a doll."

"You plan to go ahead with Friday's event?" Chambrun asked.

Lazar raised a hand to stroke his long, curly hair. "It's hard to think of going on," he said. "I remember, when President Kennedy was assassinated, I thought it was the end of the world. But after a day of mourning it was business as usual. The investment is enormous. We have models under contract who will not be available at another time. Nikos would have wanted us to go ahead. He planned for it in case anything happened to him. Rosey would feel the same way, I think."

"It's nice for you that you can justify," Chambrun said. "You think Mrs. Faraday is somewhere else in the hotel?"

"I don't know who's left in the bedroom," Monica said.

Chambrun made a little gesture with his hand and I went to see. The look-alikes were still on the bed, both of them asleep now. On a chair in the corner, his gray head bent, was Zach Chambers. He had forgotten about Merle Oberon. He was crying like a small child, tears streaming down his face, his whole body convulsed with sobs. Kneeling beside him was a gorgeous girl who must be, I thought, the one Jan had referred to as looking like Julie Christie.

"Zach, you mustn't!" she kept saying over and over.

"She was so special," Chambers choked out. "So not bitchy. She was so clean and healthy, so attractive and sporty—like a—like a Cristina Ford or a Happy Rockefeller. Not all bedroomy and sexy—but blooming. Oh, God, Laura, I loved her so much—in a very special way. I'd have let a truck run over me if she'd asked. She never treated me as though I was some kind of faggoty worm from under a rock. She treated me like I was just like anyone else. Oh, God!"

"You mustn't cry, Zach," Laura pleaded.

There was no one else in the room. I tried the john to be sure. Dodo was among the missing. I went back to report.

Chambrun was still standing with Monica and Max Lazar. I told him Dodo was gone.

"You'll probably find her in the Blue Lagoon," Lazar said. "It's her favorite place to dine. She's asked me many times, but unfortunately I have never been able to accept—thanks to you, Mr. Chambrun."

Chambrun's eyebrows rose.

"Silly rule about neckties," Lazar said. "To me neckties are an abortion. That Spanish grandee who presides over the Blue Lagoon stands guard over your Victorian tastes, Mr. Chambrun."

"There has to be someplace in the hotel where gentlemen won't be embarrassed because they're not wearing beads," Chambrun said. He looked at me. "Miss Strong tells me that outbursts of maniacal rage are part of Faraday's history. It seems his custom is to buy his way out of trouble when the storm clears."

"There was a waiter in a Paris restaurant," Lazar said. "A wheelchair case as a result. Mike settled a huge sum on him to avoid criminal prosecution." He gave me a tired smile. "You may have found a way to get rich, Haskell."

"Faraday is headed for a new experience," Chambrun said, his face grim. "I think we should find Mrs. Faraday, Mark. She may save us time."

We left the dead party and whooshed down in an express elevator to the lobby. Chambrun wasn't in a mood for conversation. As we walked away from the elevator and started toward the Blue Lagoon, Mike Maggio, the night bell captain, waylaid us. Mike has the old-young face of a Sicilian bandit.

"Been trying to find you, Mr. Chambrun," he said. "Jerry says to tell you he's got the Faraday dame in the front office."

As usual, Jerry wasn't behind the times. There is a small office back of the reception desk in the main lobby. It isn't used by anyone in particular. It's a place to take a guest who has a complaint or wants a check cashed, or to interview the banquet manager about a party. It's simply furnished with a flat-topped desk, several small upholstered armchairs, the wall decorated with photographs of famous persons and parties dating back over the years.

Dodo Faraday was sitting in one of the chairs, her hands locked tightly together in her lap. That odd, hazy, drunken look had left her. She was staring straight ahead at the wall. Jerry was sitting on the edge of the desk fiddling with a cigarette. He glanced up as we came in.

"I thought Mrs. Faraday might cut some corners for us," he said, "but she's not being very cooperative."

"I was taken away from my dinner, like a criminal," Dodo said, "brought in here, and—" She stopped. I had come into her line of vision. "Oh, my God!" she said. "Mike did that to you?"

"And my secretary—a woman—is in the hospital with a broken jaw and a possible fractured skull," Chambrun said. "I recommend to you that you help, Mrs. Faraday."

"Please," she said. "I've been so angry I haven't really been listening to what he's been saying." She nodded toward Jerry. "What is it you want me to do?"

"Gloves off, Mrs. Faraday," Chambrun said. "We understand your husband's having an affair with a girl named Jan Morse."

Her voice turned bitter. "Oh, it's on the electric sign around the Times Building every night," she said. "The whole world knows. Except Nikos. Poor Nikos. They managed to keep it from him."

"The police discovered that Rosemary Lewis jumped or was thrown from the window in Jan Morse's room," Chambrun said. "Mark took Miss Morse down to my office to wait while the police went over her room on the nineteenth floor. Your husband appeared there, Mrs. Faraday, slugged my secretary, who tried to intercept him, broke into my office and beat Mark into unconsciousness. Then he left the hotel—with Jan Morse. Where would he be likely to take her?"

"Oh, God," she said, and lowered her eyes.

"Apparently the girl went with him willingly. She wasn't dragged out by the hair of her head, Mrs. Faraday. Where would they be likely to go?"

Dodo looked up slowly, and two great tears rolled down her cheeks. "You'd think I'd be ready to help to get back at him," she said. "You're wondering why I didn't tell Nikos, who could have destroyed them both. You're wondering why Jan went off with him, not protesting, leaving two badly hurt people behind."

"I just want to find him, Mrs. Faraday," Chambrun said.

"Because I'm afraid for my life—and so is Jan," Dodo said. She looked at me. "Maybe Mr. Haskell can tell you what he's like. Mike is an unbelievable sadist, Mr. Chambrun. If I told you the things he's done to me, you wouldn't believe me. I've wanted to run, to leave him, to go to the other side of the world. It wouldn't be any use. He'd follow me, he'd find me, and in the end he'd kill me. If I wasn't afraid to die, I'd run the risk. That's why Jan went with him, in the face of everything. She knew if she didn't, she'd be confronted with—with God knows what."

"That makes it all the more urgent for us to find him," Chambrun said.

"I can only tell you what you'd find out without my help," she said. "We have a house at Fifth Avenue and Ninetieth Street."

"He'd take another woman there?"

Her laughter had a jangling sound to it. "The house has been full of women for all of our married lives!" she said. "I meet them in the hallways. I find them in my breakfast room. They don't laugh at me. They've found out that Mike is no laughing matter."

"Did you ever see Jan there?" I asked.

"No, Mike had to play it cautiously with her because of Nikos."

"Does Jan Morse have a place in town of her own?"

"Didn't you know, Mr. Chambrun? Jan Morse was Nikos's property. Where he lived, she lived. If there was anyplace she'd call home, it would be Nikos's yacht, which is anchored somewhere in the Hudson."

"Would they go there?"

Dodo shook her head. "She was Nikos's girl. The Greek pirates who run the yacht for Nikos would tear Mike apart if they found him fooling with Nikos's girl."

"Even after Nikos was dead?"

"Nikos is not dead to the people who loved him, Mr. Chambrun," Dodo said. "I wasn't one of his favorites or I might have gone to him for help. He was a man you could count on in trouble. I've heard you know that, Mr. Chambrun."

"I knew it very well," Chambrun said. "I'm sorry to put you through this, Mrs. Faraday, but we've got to find your husband." He turned to me. "Let's try the Fifth Avenue house."

My instant reaction was to plead a previous engagement. I could visualize Faraday taking both Chambrun and me apart without too much difficulty. I wasn't prepared to face him again just yet. I should have known that Chambrun wasn't going to play hero.

We had company on the way uptown in a taxi in the person of Lieutenant Hardy. The big, broad-shouldered Homicide man was a comforting presence. As we squeezed together in the back seat of the taxi, I could feel the hard shape of his gun pressed against my arm.

"I am charging him with criminal assault for the moment," Chambrun said. "Among the fingerprints your men have picked up in Jan Morse's room are going to be Faraday's. We know he spent some time there late this afternoon. That should be enough to hold him on suspicion of homicide. A man who could run amok as Faraday did in my office could be triggered to toss a woman out a window without giving it a second thought."

"I'll take him in," Hardy said cheerfully. "He'll probably produce some expensive legal talent."

Chambrun's face was turned to watch the dark tree shapes in Central Park. "I have a lot of friends in this town in key positions," he said. "I haven't spent my life asking them for irritating favors. When I do ask for the key to the jailhouse, I think I'll get it."

I'd seen the house on Fifth Avenue many times without knowing that it belonged to Faraday. It was one of the last of the old mansions that had resisted the assault of new, towering apartment buildings. It was a gray stone affair, about five stories tall. The front door, massive oak, looked as if it had been built for a medieval castle.

I don't know what I expected, but it wasn't what happened. Hardy rang the front doorbell and started reaching in his pocket for the leather case in which he carries his police badge. The door opened before he got it out. We were confronted by a man in a white house coat.

"Come in, gentlemen," he said. "Mr. Faraday is expecting you."

We looked at each other, wondering.

We were led across a great entrance hall, thickly carpeted, gloomy portraits of Faraday's ancestors peering down at us from the walls—and into a living room that belonged in another world. The furnishings were the most modern of modern—chromium, angles, a white fur rug before a huge white marble fireplace, a dozen garish pop-art paintings on the walls. At the far end of the room was an elaborate bar, stacked with bottles and expensive-looking glass. Faraday was standing by it, a drink in his hand. He was wearing white silk house pajamas, cut in a version of a karate expert's uniform. There were rope sandals on his feet. His perpetually suntanned skin was handsomely set off by the white silk and the white and silver scheme of the room. He gave us a cordial, almost warm smile.

"I've been expecting you, gentlemen," he said. "My wife phoned me that you were on the way. How are you, Chambrun?" He frowned sympathetically. "I hope things aren't too bad with you, Haskell." The pale eyes moved to Hardy. "I assume this gentleman is from the police."

Dodo Faraday was so frightened of him she'd had to warn him.

"Lieutenant Hardy, Homicide," our Notre Dame fullback said. "I'm here to arrest you on charges of criminal assault and suspicion of homicide."

Faraday's face clouded. "The secretary?" he asked.

"My secretary is in the intensive care unit at the hospital," Chambrun said. "God help you if she doesn't make it. The homicide charge at the moment relates to Rosemary Lewis."

"Oh, come on!" Faraday said. "You think I tossed Rosey out a window? How absurd can you get?"

"You're aware of your legal rights," Hardy said. "You're entitled to counsel from your attorney. You don't need to answer questions. But I'm booking you. Would you like to change your clothes before I take you downtown?"

The Faraday mask was completely amiable and undisturbed. "Before we go formal, can I make you gentlemen a drink?"

"Is Miss Morse here in the house with you?" Hardy asked. "I want her, too."

"Jan? No, she's not here."

"I can get a search warrant in about ten minutes," Hardy said.

"My dear fellow, you don't need a warrant," Faraday said. "You're free to look anywhere you like. But I tell you Jan isn't here."

"She left the hotel with you," Chambrun said.

"True. But we separated shortly afterwards. We had a drink at some little dump down the street from the Beaumont. Then Jan went back to the hotel and I came home."

"She went back to the hotel?"

"That's where she said she was going. Isn't she there?" The pale eyes glittered as he looked at me. "She was worried about you, Haskell. I—I'm sorry about the whole thing. I just blew my stack. And your secretary, Chambrun—I just gave her a little push and she fell and struck her head on the desk. I didn't think—"

"That little push broke her jaw," Chambrun said.

Faraday shook his head regretfully. "When I get turned on, I sometimes don't realize that I'm a little too rough. Of course I'll pay all the lady's doctor bills, hospital, a reasonable period for recuperation anywhere she'd like to go."

"You bet you will," Chambrun said.

"As for you, Haskell," Faraday said, smiling, "put a reasonable price on your wounded feelings and I'll meet it without argument."

"The courts will determine the amount of damages," Hardy said. "Be good enough to change your clothes, unless you prefer to go downtown as you are."

"Let's try to be a little bit reasonable," Faraday said. "I'm ready to be completely cooperative, Lieutenant. I might even be a little helpful about the mess at the Beaumont."

"You and Miss Morse walked out of the hotel," Chambrun said, "leaving two people unconscious in my office. You didn't try to get help for either of them. You just sauntered out and went down the street for a drink."

"I realize that must be hard for you to understand," Faraday said.

"Impossible," Chambrun said.

"I've been cursed, ever since I was a small boy, with a violent temper. I—well, when I take off, I have no control over what happens. Jan knows me. She knows how I am. The best thing to do was to get me away from there, and she managed it somehow. She knew if I stayed there I might take off again. So—so she got me out of the hotel, and I managed to cool off, and then she went back to the hotel to help. It was the best thing for her to do—to get me away."

"If she came back to the hotel, none of us is aware of it," Chambrun said.

"What the hell got into you?" I asked, not able to hold back any longer.

He looked at me, and I saw a little nerve twitch high up on his brown cheek. "Jan is my girl," he said. "But I know how she is and how any man will react to her line. When I heard you'd taken her down to Chambrun's office—well, I saw red."

"So you slugged Miss Ruysdale," Chambrun said.

"When I'm like that," Faraday said, "nobody had better get in my way."

"The world is crawling with anarchists of one kind or another these days," Chambrun said. "Your kind, Faraday, ought to be locked up permanently for the sake of community safety. Know that I'm going to have a try at it."

"Surely we can work this out reasonably," Faraday said.

"So cooperate," Hardy said. "I'm dealing with two apparent homicides at the Beaumont. What do you know about them?"

You could almost see the wheels turning behind Faraday's brown forehead.

"The world of Nikos Karados," he said. "You call me an anarchist, Chambrun, because I take a slug at anyone who stands in my way. Your friend Nikos was one on a much bigger scale. He destroyed whole businesses, even governments in his time. Cross him on the smallest detail and you were promptly crushed, while he sat in his big armchair drinking milk and grinning at you. Power, used the whole length of the scale, from financing a revolution to upsetting a government that didn't please him, to stepping on a spider that happened to intrude on his living quarters." There were little beads of sweat on Faraday's upper lip, and he blotted at them with a handkerchief he produced from the sleeve of his pajama top. "If I knew that Nikos was going to find out something about me that would displease him, I'd use every resource I had to disappear, to dissolve, to evaporate. I am a rich man. Nikos could buy and sell me twenty times over. Not anyone survived Nikos's anger. I tell you this because you must be thinking of people who will inherit handsomely now that he's dead; people like Tim Gallivan, and Monica Strong, and Max Lazar, and Zach Chambers."

"And Jan Morse," Chambrun said.

"Yes—and Jan. But I tell you the motive could lie somewhere else. Not the anticipation of money, but the fear of Nikos's revenge." The pale eyes glittered. "Nikos owned people. Do you think Jan could go to him and say, 'Good-by, Nikos, baby. I've decided to make a life with Mike Faraday'? Do you think she was free to make such a decision? Never, unless by luck he happened to be tired of her and was glad to have her go. But if he wanted to keep her, God help her if she tried to go."

"You're supplying both yourself and Miss Morse with a motive," Hardy said.

Faraday's smile was white and mirthless. "Sure I am, because anyone connected with Nikos had a motive. There were dozens of us. Max Lazar, an independent creative genius, got caught in the trap. Nikos had to approve any design he made. Cross Nikos, and he was dead in the fashion field. Monica Strong has to run her business Nikos's way, or else. Even the models Zach Chambers supplies—let one of them pose for another client in a way that was distasteful to Nikos, like a nudie picture for *Playboy* or some kind of commercial underwear schmaltz, and she was done in the field forever—

and Zach would feel the great man's wrath, too. It sounds absurd, but if Nikos was sore at the people who make cornflakes, you better damn well not eat them for breakfast. The woods are full of people who were afraid of the Big Crackdown. Don't look for impatient heirs. If you were enough of a favorite to be in Nikos's will, you didn't have to be impatient. Ask and ye shall receive, was his motto. You didn't have to be in a hurry."

"I'm sick of this picture some of you draw of Nikos as a destructive monster," Chambrun said, his voice harsh. "I knew him more intimately and under greater pressures than most of you. Yes, he destroyed businesses. So do the big chain groceries destroy the little store owners. Yes, he destroyed governments by withdrawing his aid or attacking their financial structures. So does the United States government. Yes, he stopped feeding friends through a golden funnel when they displeased him or tried to use him. I do the same thing. He was a generous man, a kind man, a man you could count on to the hilt in a pinch. What did you want of him? That he should supply you with handouts to support some project he didn't believe in or care for? No, Faraday. The person who killed Nikos and then threw Rosemary Lewis out a window is the villain of this piece, not Nikos." Chambrun turned to Hardy. "I think I'd like this place searched for Jan Morse, Lieutenant. I don't care for her taste in men, but she can be in real danger and I don't propose to let something happen to her as a result of our negligence."

"With or without a search warrant?" Hardy asked Faraday.

"Oh, I'll take you on the guided tour, Lieutenant," Faraday said, smiling his white smile, "but it will take some time. This is a rather large house, going from wine cellar to attic. I assure you Jan isn't here, but if my word isn't good enough—"

"Your word isn't worth a damn, Faraday," Chambrun said. He turned to me. "Go back to the hotel, Mark, and start the wheels turning there. It's possible she went back to the hotel without being seen. Just barely possible."

3

I FOUND A TAXI without too much difficulty and headed back for the Beaumont. I noticed the driver kept glancing at me in his rear-view mirror.

"You look like you could use a plastic surgeon," he said finally.

"I bumped into a door," I said.

"He must have been a big sonofabitch," the driver said.

"Big and crazy," I said.

The driver nodded. "You aren't the first guy I ever drove away from that house with a thick lip," he said. "What the hell goes on there? Some kind of masochists' club?"

"Don't tell me," I said. "You're a college professor moonlighting as a cab driver at night."

He grinned. "Something like that. I'm an actor. You learn quite a lot about this town driving at night. Places people go —and stay." He pulled to a stop for a red light. "People as rich as Faraday can buy themselves out of almost anything. I had him on a ride to the airport once. We got talking and he found out I was an actor." The light changed and we cruised on down the Avenue. "He told me he could put me next to some guy who was making underground films. You know, sex games in the nude for the stag trade. He talked interesting money, but it wasn't my dish of tea. Every once in a while when the going gets pretty tough I wonder if I made a mistake. I've cruised around the house back there, but I never got him for a fare again, and he never told me where I should go to apply for the job."

"Who else have you seen beat up?" I said, touching my bruised cheekbone gently.

"Who knows who? But every once in a while someone comes out of there bloody but unbowed. I figured it was Queer Street. You don't look the type."

"Thanks," I said.

"You live at the Beaumont?"

"I work there."

"I just heard on the radio that some dame took a dive out a nineteenth-story window."

"That's how I got hurt," I said. "Trying to catch her."

He was right. The Faradays of this world can get away with almost anything. I paid him off under the canopy and told him if he was ever really thirsty, if he'd ask for me I'd buy him a drink. I walked into the hotel, wondering what *did* go on in Faraday's house in addition to his women and his sadistic treatment of his wife. Chambrun was on target when he said that kind of anarchist should be permanently put away.

I got a few crude remarks from Nevers, the night reception clerk, when he saw my face. But he located Jerry Dodd for me. He was with Hardy's men, who were putting the partygoers on the grill up in 19A. Jerry met me in the corridor outside the suite. He looked angry.

"Any luck?" I asked him.

"You never heard such jabbering in your life," he said. "Everybody loved Karados. Nobody saw anything. Everybody loved Rosey. Nobody saw anything."

"Unless you had a reason for keeping tabs on someone, it wasn't the kind of party where you'd notice comings and goings," I said. "I couldn't give you a very clear account of who was where while I was present."

"What's on your mind?" Jerry asked.

"Jan Morse. She wasn't with Faraday. At least he says she's not there, but the boss and Hardy are searching the house. Faraday isn't objecting, so I assume they won't find her. Faraday says she came back to the hotel about a half hour after she went out with him. The boss wants her found and stayed by."

"She's not in there or in her room," Jerry said. "Homicide boys are still in nineteen hundred seven."

"You better alert the staff to start looking—all over," I said.

"Where will you be?"

"In my apartment trying to get cleaned up a little," I said. "Then I'll start wandering."

"Check," Jerry said. A faint smile moved his mouth. "Was she worth that beating, Mark?"

"You go to your church and I'll go to mine," I said.

I went down to my apartment on the fourth floor, stripped down, and stood under the shower. It felt good. I had a lot of sore spots that relished the gentle hotness. Jerry's impudent question had started me thinking about Jan in other terms than where was she. She wasn't the first exposure I'd ever had to an eager dame, and I'm not blowing up my masculine attraction when I say that. In my job I've been pushed in the path of an endless stream of innocent-looking nymphos. There are the very young who can't wait to get started, the middle-aged grass widows who are rather tragically desperate, and the out-and-out sex nuts of all ages. I'm there. My job entails politeness, stretched to the *n*th degree. I've learned all the negative gambits.

Jan was different than anyone else I could remember. There'd been nothing coy or arch about her. She'd been direct and honest about her particular code. I guess a lot of the kids fifteen years younger than I am are the same way, only they don't have the money to patronize the Beaumont. They aren't surrounded by all the cliches that controlled my young life. In my day pre-marital or extra-marital sex provided you with a one-way ticket down the shoot to eternal damnation. The kids today don't think about it at all in terms of right and wrong. If you want it, you take it, with no more thought than you would give to buying a Coke if you were thirsty. Immoral, amoral—you name it. My generation winks at alcoholism, which destroys more people and more homes than anything else in the country. We wink at the hundreds of thousands of deaths and cripplings caused by lung cancer. We like to smoke, so we ignore the warnings and the facts. But sex, the most natural of all man's hungers, is surrounded by rigid rules and considered a vice if those rules aren't obeyed. The new youth may have something, I thought. They cut through a lot of hypocrisy, at any rate.

I hardly knew Jan Morse, and yet I found myself stirred by her and concerned for her. I'd seen her in crisis, and I hadn't a doubt in the world she'd really cared for Nikos—not just for his money. I'd seen her fight for his life. She'd been loyal to him in her terms, Faraday or no Faraday. I'd seen the reactions to her, even in her own crowd—Monica Strong, Tim

Gallivan, Dodo Faraday. She was a no-good tramp because she was uninhibited about her sex life. But she was loyal, and honest, and direct, which was more then could be said about her critics—and most other people. For those very reasons I had to agree with Chambrun that she was in danger. She was trying to find out who had shifted Nikos's pills, and we had to believe, because of what had happened to Rosey Lewis, that the boom would be lowered on her if she only got within whiffing distance of the truth. She had to be gotten under Chambrun's protective wing.

In clean, fresh clothes I felt better and looked better. The mark on my cheek and the slightly swollen eye above it weren't too sensationally noticeable, and the swelling on my lower lip had subsided. I was just loading myself with the final necessities—wallet, handkerchief, lighter, cigarettes—when my phone rang. It was Chambrun.

"As far as we can tell, the girl isn't at Faraday's," he said. "Any news there?"

"Not yet. Jerry's working on it. Where are you?"

"Precinct house. Faraday's being booked, fingerprinted, the works. Legal help is on the way, and I am about to call on friends to help combat it. But I had an idea, Mark."

"Yes?"

"The photographer. What's his name?"

"Stein. Morrie Stein."

"He was taking pictures all over the bedroom, you told me. Miles of film shot from all angles. It's possible that in all that picture-taking he may, quite unintentionally, have caught Miss Lewis going into Jan's room, and perhaps the person who went in after her. Get hold of him and get him to develop his film and show you what he got."

"Right."

"And tell Jerry looking for the Morse girl is not just hide-

and-seek. I'm worried for her."

"Right."

I took off for the 19th floor and Nikos's suite. The door wasn't on the latch any more and a plainclothes cop answered my ring. Beyond him in the room I saw our man Cameron. I was admitted when Cameron gave the cop a confirming nod. One of Hardy's boys, a detective sergeant named Jansen, was apparently doing the questioning. He was working on the girl who looked like Julie Christie. He didn't pay any attention to me.

I told Joe Cameron what Chambrun wanted.

"They're through with Stein," Joe said. His smile had a bitter twist to it. "Practically had to drag him out of here. I always knew Chambrun had ESP."

"What do you mean?"

"Everyone else takes off out of this suite on the run when Jansen is through with them," Joe said. "Not Stein. Ten guesses why he didn't want to leave."

"I give up," I said.

"Someone swiped his camera and his film case," Joe said. "Stein insisted we should forget about murder and turn the mice loose to find his equipment. Maby there was something on film. He took over three hundred pictures in that bedroom. But they're gone."

Part Three

1

IT SEEMED IMPORTANT enough for Joe Cameron to interrupt Jansen. The sergeant was a tall, thin man with thinning gray hair and opaque gray eyes that told you nothing. He looked mildly irritated when Joe mentioned Stein until he got to the point.

"The film he used up, which was in the film case, and the roll in the camera could be important," Joe said. "Maybe we should worry about Stein's equipment, after all."

Jansen nodded. "Chambrun's right. There could have been a shot of something Stein wouldn't remember because he was concentrating on something else. He's been on the grill, you know. Denies he saw the Lewis dame go into the next room—or anyone else. But the camera could have caught something he wasn't trying to get."

"He said he put his stuff down on the bureau in the bedroom while he went to the john," Joe said. "When he came out, the camera and the film case were gone. He thought someone was teasing him. Apparently he gets to be the butt of a lot of practical joke kidding. You heard him talk, Mark?"

"No. Just close one eye and click the camera."

"He's on the wild side," Joe said. "No sense of humor. The In-people enjoy ribbing him. He knows it. He thought someone had moved the camera to provoke him. His word—'provoke.' When it didn't turn up, he began to yell like a stuck pig."

"So now we need a witness who saw the camera taken," I said.

"Will try," Jansen said, "but everybody at this goddam party seems to have been educated in the practice of noticing nothing. One'll get you five Stein hasn't left the hotel, Mr. Haskell. He isn't going to leave here till he finds his precious equipment."

I found Morrie Stein in the Trapeze Bar. He was sitting on one of the upholstered stools at the bar itself, face buried in his hands, bent over a vodka and tonic. His long dark hair had fallen down over his eyes. He had on a seersucker jacket over his blue turtle-neck sweater. The tight black pants looked ready to split at the seams.

I paused a few stools down the mahogany counter, and Eddie, the night bar captain, came over to me.

"Friend of yours?" he asked, seeing my interest in Stein.

"Part of the trouble on nineteen," I said.

"Don't bump into him," Eddie said. "He'll fall off the stool. Last two drinks have been the eyedropper variety. He's too stoned to notice."

"I want to talk to him," I said. "If I offer to buy him a drink, don't flinch. And you can bring me a Jack Daniels—"

"—on the rocks," Eddie said.

I moved along and took the stool next to Stein. "I'd like to talk to you, Morrie," I said.

He lifted his head and turned it. Through the lock of hair I saw his bloodshot eyes. He had, for God sake, been crying. Tears seemed to come easy in the world of Nikos Karados.

"Who the hell are you?" he asked.

"Mark Haskell, public relations director for the hotel. I'm concerned about the loss of your camera. We don't take thefts in the hotel lightly."

"Well, I should hope not!" he said. He tapped his empty glass on the bar. "Fill her up again, man," he said. "I want to tell you one thing, Haskell. If I don't get my films back, you're going to hear about it, but plenty. The camera is bad enough. But it's insured; it can be replaced. But nobody can replace those pictures I took. Nine and a half rolls, for God sake! Damn near three hundred and thirty pictures."

"What kind of a camera was it, Morrie?" I asked.

"Leica—thirty-five millimeter," he said. "With all the stuff I had on it—closeup lens, wide-angle lens—it was probably worth a thousand clams. But the film is what can't be replaced. You couldn't place a value on it. Why, I may have got something there—something of Suzie, for example—that could be *the* picture of the year; of the century, even!"

"I'm interested in that film, too, Morrie," I said.

"Interested enough to find it, I hope," he said. "So help me, if someone is just playing a mean joke on me—"

"I don't think it's that, Morrie," I said.

"You don't know them," he said. "They're always cooking up something that'll start me screaming. Oh, I scream when I get annoyed. I really scream. They think it's funny, damn them."

Eddie brought the drinks, and when Morrie tried to reach for money, I told him it was on the house. "Mind if I ask you a couple of technical questions, Morrie?"

"Could I stop you?" he said, and took a big swig of his nothing-drink. "I must be bombing out. Can't taste the liquor any more."

"I saw you working in the bedroom of nineteen-A," I said, "taking shots of Suzie and her boy from all different angles."

He smiled dreamily. "Aren't they beautiful? Two most beautiful kids I ever saw."

"Did you use your closeup lens for all of that?" I asked him.

"Closeup and wide-angle both," he said. "Wide angle you catch other people in the background. Makes it look not posed, if you see what I mean."

I tried to take it easy. "They asked you questions upstairs," I said. "Like, did you see Rosey Lewis go into Jan's room, and did you see anyone else follow her in there?"

"I told them a thousand times I didn't!" he said, his voice rising. "I was concentrating on Suzie and Tommy. I didn't give a damn about anything else."

"When you used your wide-angle lens, do you know what was in the background?" I asked.

"Not till I develop the film," he said.

"Then it's just possible that somewhere in those three hundred and thirty pictures you took Rosey Lewis might be in the background and the person who followed her into Jan's room, too. You wouldn't know till you developed the film."

He stared at me, his red-rimmed eyes widened.

"It's possible you took a picture of the murderer without knowing it," I said. "I think that's why your camera was taken, Morrie. Not a practical joke."

"Oh, my God," he said, "then I won't get them back!"

Rosey didn't matter. Nothing mattered to him except he'd lost his pictures of those "two most beautiful kids."

"If we found the films, Morrie," I said, "how long would it

take you to develop them—so we could look at something?"

He shrugged. "My dark room assistant could develop and print them on a contact sheet for you in an hour, maybe less. But you're not going to find them!" His voice rose in a wail that had heads turning. "You'll never find them!"

"Now that we know how important they are, we may get a lead," I said.

But I knew we weren't going to find his film. If we were right, the killer had long since exposed them to destructive light.

Morrie, his face the mask of tragedy, was looking past me toward the entrance. He raised his arm in a limp gesture of greeting. I turned to look and saw a man who would have been an eye-stopper in any room anyplace in the world. He must have been only just a little under seven feet tall. He was no skinny basketball freak. Every inch of his towering frame was muscled. He was wearing a sort of blue uniform, brass buttons on the double-breasted jacket, and carrying a white yachting cap in huge hands. His height wasn't the only thing about him to attract attention. I rarely find myself impelled to use the word "beautiful" in describing a man, but this was something out of a classic sculpture concept. His hair was black, thick, and curling against the head of a god. His skin was sun- and wind-tanned to a rich mahogany-brown. And his face! It had the perfect symmetry of something carved on a coin—intellectual forehead, aquiline nose, firm jaw, a strong wide mouth. I remembered photographs I'd seen of a young John Barrymore in the role of Hamlet, only this giant yachtsman would have made two of Barrymore in size.

He was coming across the room toward us.

"Who's your friend?" I asked Morrie Stein.

"Isn't he something?" Morrie said. "I've taken hundreds of pictures of him. He could make a million in the movies with that face and body—and you should hear his voice. But no, he's stuck to Nikos. Maybe it will pay off."

"But who is he?"

"Gorgeous George, the girls call him," Morrie said.

The giant was beside us. "Hello, Mr. Stein," he said. His voice was deep, rich, musical, faintly accented. "I've been trying to find Mr. Gallivan, but his room phone doesn't answer."

Morrie nodded toward me. "This is Haskell. He's the hotel's PR man. Maybe he can help you. Oh, God, isn't everything awful!"

The giant smiled at me. "I am George Pappas," he said. "I am the captain of Mr. Karados's yacht."

We shook hands.

"The police are pretty much in charge upstairs," I said. "That probably explains why Gallivan's phone doesn't answer. I could try to find him for you if it's important."

Pappas looked at Eddie and asked for a straight vodka in a shot glass. No ice. "We only heard the word on the radio a little while ago about Mr. Karados," he said. "Of course we've all known it would happen, sooner or later, but it was a great shock to all of us." He was talking about death from angina, not murder. "I have been with Mr. Karados since I was a small boy—cabin boy on the *Merina*, as a matter of fact. My father was captain. Serving Mr. Karados has been my whole life." He picked up the drink Eddie brought him and swallowed it in one deep-throated gulp. "May he rest in peace. And then we got the word about Miss Lewis. Incredible. She was a guest on the *Merina* many times. A wonderful woman. It is hard to believe."

I turned to Eddie and asked him to call Joe Cameron in 19A and have him tell Gallivan that Captain Pappas was here to see him.

"I don't know if the word is on the radio yet that Miss

Lewis wasn't a suicide," I said to Pappas.

His eyes darkened. "I could have sworn to that," he said. "She was too fond of living, too full of life. I would like to get my hands on whoever is responsible."

"Nikos didn't go easily, either," Morrie Stein said. "The word is he was poisoned, George."

Pappas looked at me. I knew then and there I didn't want him as an enemy. "This is true?" he asked me.

"He died of a heart attack," I said. "But it's not much of a secret any more that someone tampered with his medicine. When he needed it, there was nothing in his little green bottle to help him. Bicarbonate. He was helped along."

Pappas brought his huge fist down on the bar and I thought he was going to shatter it. He muttered something under his breath in Greek. It sounded more profane than any familiar Anglo-Saxon expletive.

"The police are aware?"

"Naturally."

"This cannot be allowed to happen!" Pappas said. "This cannot go unpunished!"

"That's the general theory," I said. "The police and Mr. Chambrun, my boss, are determined."

"Mr. Chambrun was Mr. Karados's great good friend," Pappas said. "I would like to talk to him."

"He's out of the hotel at the moment," I said. I looked at this giant and thought he must know of many secrets in Nikos's private life. The yacht *Merina* had been a sort of home base for Nikos for many years. The famous and the infamous had been its guests. I thought of Jan, and asked the natural question.

"We're concerned about Jan Morse," I said. "We can't find her. She hasn't visited the *Merina* this evening, has she?"

"Miss Jan? But no! She has a permanent cabin on the boat;

she's free to come and go. But she hasn't been aboard for several days. How do you mean, you can't find her?"

I told him, briefly, what had happened with Faraday. "He says she came back to the hotel from a little bar where they were drinking. No one here has seen her. Mr. Chambrun is concerned. She could be in danger, as Miss Lewis was."

"Faraday!" Pappas said, clenching his huge fists. "I have always dreamed he might explode at me one day. I would have the excuse to take him apart, limb from limb."

"You know Jan well?" I asked, wondering if this beautiful male had ever been offered Jan's gift to mankind.

"She has been permanently on the *Merina* for the last two years," Pappas said. "A wonderful girl, Mr. Haskell. She made Mr. Karados immensely happy. Do you need help in finding her? I have twelve men aboard the *Merina*. We will take apart the city of New York if you ask it."

"It's a large place to take apart, Captain," I said. "For the moment I think the most we'll ask you to do is let us know if she turns up at the *Merina*. If she does, hang onto her until someone comes to get her. She shouldn't be running around unprotected."

"You can count on it," Pappas said. "I will call the *Merina* at once. Ship to shore phone."

I gestured to Eddie. "Give the Captain a telephone," I said.

The phone appeared on the bar, jacked in. Pappas dialed a number. Presently he began to talk, volubly, in Greek. He finally put down the phone and pushed it away from him.

"She hasn't come to the *Merina* since I came ashore," he said. "But my men have orders to call you if she does, and to detain her until they have instructions from you."

"Many thanks," I said, not feeling hopeful. The chance that she might have gone to the yacht after leaving Faraday had been a long shot.

At that moment Tim Gallivan came across the room toward us. I was a little shocked by his appearance. He'd changed out of his mod gear into a plain charcoal-gray suit, with white shirt and black knitted tie. The bounce seemed to have gone out of him. He looked tired and old.

"Hello, George," he said to Pappas. He looked at Morrie Stein with something like distaste. "You better paddle upstairs, Morrie. They've found your stuff."

"Found it!" Morrie shouted. "How wonderful!"

"Not so wonderful for you, friend," Gallivan said. "It was all in the trash can outside the freight elevator on that floor. Miles of film, exposed, destroyed. Your camera looks as if it might still take pictures, but there's nothing in it."

"Oh, God!" Morrie said, and he hurried away, yelping like a wounded animal.

Gallivan asked Eddie for a Scotch on the rocks. "Black day, George," he said to Pappas.

"Hard to believe," Pappas said.

The crow's-feet around Gallivan's eyes looked as if they'd been etched in with an engraver's tool. "You haven't found Jan yet, Mark?" he asked me.

"Not yet."

He ran a hand over his eyes as if they ached. "I try to keep from believing it," he said. "I keep assuring the police that, next to me, she was Nikos's most trusted friend. Knowing her, I tell myself it's impossible."

"What's impossible?"

Gallivan looked at me steadily with his tired, lifeless eyes. "Sooner or later, however decent his intentions, man is corrupted by his private sickness, whatever it may be—drink, drugs, sexual deviation. Sooner or later his need to satisfy these destructive appetites makes him unreliable. Jan's sickness —well, it's no secret, is it, Mark? An insatiable sexual appetite.

I believe she was genuinely fond of Nikos; I believe she was completely loyal to him in every way but one. But she was finally corrupted by Faraday. I don't blame Faraday. We've all been offered her golden gift. You, George, it happened to you, too, didn't it?"

Pappas nodded. "I laughed at her," he said. "She was Mr. Karados's property."

"There it is," Gallivan said. He took a deep swallow of his Scotch as though he needed it badly. "Her sickness overcame her loyalty. So I say to myself, she had the most easy access to Nikos's medicine; Rosey was killed and thrown from the window in her room. I have to wonder if that isn't why she is missing."

My mouth felt dry. "You mean she's running away from the police?"

Gallivan shrugged. "It sounds fancy," he said, "but perhaps she's running away from herself. She arranged for Nikos to die, because the whispers about her were growing louder. He was bound to get wind of the truth. Would you believe she wanted him to die, not to save herself a fortune, but to keep him from being hurt by the truth? It could be that intricate, Mark. It could be—with her twisted concept of loyalty. Then Rosey stumbled on the truth and Jan had to act on the spur of the moment. Now—now she is living with a horror of herself and what she has done. She has disappeared to think it out." He finished his drink and put the empty glass down on the bar. "It will not surprise me if, when she is found, she will not have inflicted her own punishment on herself."

"You are suggesting—?" Pappas began.

"—that we may not find her alive," Gallivan said. He signaled to Eddie for another Scotch. "How to go about finding her? She can have checked into any one of a thousand hotels in New York to think things out. She's not here, not on the

Merina, the only places where she had belongings." He shook his head from side to side. "I don't want to be the one to go to the police with this notion, damn it. I'm fond of the girl. I may be doing her a wild injustice. Nikos would want me to help her, no matter what she'd done. Your Chambrun may be right; she may be hiding out of fear of someone we haven't even thought of. Will you talk it over with Chambrun, Mark? He's had more experience with this kind of thing than I have. I—I just don't want to be the one to point the finger at Jan, but I can't help the unpleasant certainty that we want her for murder and not to protect her."

I felt a sick knot at the pit of my stomach. It had never occurred to me for an instant to think of Jan as suspect. She was undisciplined, free of any moral checks, but never a cold-blooded killer. Yet the way Gallivan had put it, the shoe might fit. She might have let Nikos die with the perverted notion that she was saving him from a big hurt. Confronted with it by Rosey, she might—but there I just couldn't go along. I couldn't imagine her killing Rosey and calmly heaving the body out her window. And there was the business of Morrie Stein's camera. To the best of my knowledge Jan had never been at the party in 19A. But there was a blank in my knowledge. During the time I'd been in Chambrun's office with Rosey Lewis Jan could have been in and out of 19A a number of times without my knowing. That I needed to check on, to be certain.

"I'll talk to Chambrun," I said to Gallivan.

"Fine. It'll take the responsibility off my shoulders. If Chambrun wants me to come forward, I will. Meanwhile, George and I have a lot of business details to discuss—what's to be done with the *Merina* and its crew; other affairs that Nikos's death drops in our laps. With the police swarming over our quarters upstairs, is there someplace we can go to talk quietly? Some office somewhere?"

I suggested that little office back of the registration desk in the main lobby, and I took them down there and had Carl Nevers install them there.

"Mrs. Kiley has been trying to reach you," Nevers told me, as he took Gallivan and Captain Pappas in tow.

Mrs. Kiley is the chief night operator on the hotel switchboard. I got her on one of the house phones.

"I thought you ought to know," Mrs. Kiley said in her matter-of-fact voice. "It happened just after you and Mr. Chambrun left the hotel."

"What happened?" I asked.

"An outside call," Mrs. Kiley said, meaning it hadn't come from any phone connected with the switchboard. "A lady who didn't give her name, inquiring about you and Miss Ruysdale."

"Name?"

"She didn't give her name," Mrs. Kiley said. "She didn't ask to speak to anyone special—just asked her question of the operator, who turned the call over to me. She was concerned about you. She wanted to know what hospital Miss Ruysdale had been taken to. She obviously knew what had happened in Mr. Chambrun's office."

"And you told her?"

"That you had left the hotel. That I couldn't tell her Miss Ruysdale's whereabouts. Against policy to give addresses to anyone."

"Husky, kind of young-sounding voice?" I asked.

"I don't have a romantic ear, Mr. Haskell," Mrs. Kiley said dryly.

"You sure it was an outside call?"

"You know our system well enough to know there's no question," Mrs. Kiley said. "Outside calls came over to one set of operators, house calls to another. I can't tell you the call wasn't made in the hotel. There are dozens of private phones and coin boxes in the hotel. But it wasn't a room phone, or any of the house phones."

"Thanks, Mrs. Kiley. And if the same woman calls again, try to hang onto her until you can connect me."

"I'll try. *Are* you all right, Mr. Haskell?"

"Bruised but not broken, Mrs. Kiley."

"Dr. Partridge left a message for Mr. Chambrun," she said. "It's not the worst with Miss Ruysdale. No skull fracture."

"Good news. Thanks again. And hang onto that gal if she calls."

It had to have been Jan. What other woman knew what had happened in Chambrun's office and would be concerned? I turned away from the reception desk and saw Chambrun coming through the revolving door from the street. He had a trench coat draped over the shoulders of his dinner jacket. I was damn glad to see him.

"Faraday's been charged with criminal assault and suspicion of homicide," he said. "They'll probably have him out on bail before breakfast, but we'll keep him occupied in the meanwhile. You find Miss Morse?"

"Not yet. Jerry's got a search in hand. But—"

"Let's talk in my office," Chambrun said.

On the way up I gave him the good news about Miss Ruysdale. I could see some of the tensions in his face relax a little.

In his office he went straight to the sideboard and poured himself a demitasse of Turkish coffee and a snifter of old brandy. He gestured to me to help myself. I felt as if I'd been drinking steadily for hours. I didn't want anything.

When he'd settled in his desk armchair and got a cigarette going, I gave him the whole package, starting with the disappearance and eventual recovery of Morrie Stein's equipment, and ending with Gallivan's unhappy theory about Jan. Chambrun listened, his eyes hidden behind their hooded lids.

"You think Gallivan's theory holds water?" he asked me when I'd finished.

"I suppose it could," I said.

"You sound reluctant to accept it."

"I'll tell you the truth, sir," I said. "My judgment about her isn't very sound. In spite of everything I—I found her attractive, quite candid about her way of life, different, and—and—"

"Disturbing?" he suggested.

"Yes."

"But she did have access to the pills, it was her room, she could quite easily have removed Stein's camera and destroyed his film."

"Yes."

"But she did call in to find out if you and Ruysdale were all right. So she's a good scout."

"Yes," I said.

"And she did call us to tell us her room was the place from which Miss Lewis had been thrown. A clever way of throwing suspicion off herself, wouldn't you say?"

"I suppose so."

"On the other hand, if she was guilty, why didn't she just remove the piece of cloth from the air conditioner, close the window and keep her mouth shut?"

"Just what are you trying to say, sir?"

He chuckled. "That you can use one set of facts to prove two different stories," he said. "If you want to prove your Miss Morse is guilty, you can use the facts to bolster that theory. If you want to think she's innocent, you can use the same facts to make that stand up. Only one thing holds fast. Guilty or innocent, she's got to be found, Mark."

"She's not at either of the two places where you might say she lives," I said. "She's not on the *Merina* and she's not here."

"We don't know for certain that she's not here," Chambrun said. "She's not in any of the public rooms, or any of the rooms on the nineteenth floor occupied by the Karados party. But there are hundreds of rooms where she could be."

"Her phone call came from outside somewhere."

"There are nearly fifty outside lines in the hotel." He reached for the house phone on his desk. "Find Jerry Dodd and tell him I want to see him in my office." He leaned back in his chair and lit a fresh cigarette. "Thousands of people with thousands of complex problems have come under our roof here, Mark, in the last twenty years. I've listened to all kinds of reasons, motives, explanations for extraordinary behavior in my time. You can write down money and power at the very top of the list—and underline them. We're a luxury segment of our society. People who are dealing in peanuts don't stay at the Beaumont. I haven't seen Nikos's will, but way at the top of the heap, in terms of stakes, is our friend Gallivan. I listen to what he has to say with a little question mark at the back of my mind. He wants this mess cleared up and cleared up quickly so that he can inherit his fortune in cash and his empire in power. Nikos's estate will remain frozen until the police come up with his killer. Gallivan wants this to happen in a hurry. He'll suggest anything that might help to wrap things up."

"You think he's trying to pin this on Jan just to hurry things?" I asked.

"He'd pin it on her—or you, or me—anything to speed up the machinery," Chambrun said. "He's got his hands on a golden world and he wants to start running it. I'm not eager to buy his solutions. But I'm in a hell of a hurry to find your Jan. Guilty or innocent, she's in bad trouble."

There was a tentative knock at the office door. Jerry would have breezed in. Chambrun nodded and I went to see who it was.

Max Lazar stood outside the door. He'd put on a plaid-patterned tweed jacket over his open-necked shirt and his beads. I knew he must have taken on about a gallon of martinis since the beginning of the party in 19A, but he seemed miraculously sober. His dark eyes moved past me to Chambrun.

"I'm glad to find you both here," he said. "May I come in?"

"Of course," Chambrun said.

Lazar came in, looking around the room—at the furnishings and the paintings. "Nikos told me you were a man of taste, Chambrun," he said. "More than that, he said you were a man to whom he'd trust his life. I'm here because I need help, really from both of you."

"Sit down, Mr. Lazar," Chambrun said. "Coffee? A drink?"

"I'd be grateful for some coffee," he said. "I've been rather pouring it on all evening." He sat down in one of the high-backed Florentine chairs. I got him coffee. He sipped. "Turkish. And well made, which is a rarity," he said.

I was aware for the first time that there was an almost aristocratic bone structure to his face—strong jaw and wide mouth, high cheekbones. The long hair and the fancy costume had made me think him slightly effeminate. Perhaps his profession had bulwarked that notion; the world of male fashion designers has its share of faggoty characters.

"I have a serious decision to make," Lazar said. "It's about my showing on Friday." He put his demitasse down on the little table beside his chair. "Nikos wanted success for me. He believed in my instincts for fashion. But most of all, and having been his friend, I think you'll know I'm not downgrading him, Chambrun—most of all, he wanted to win a battle. The fashion writers and the trade journals haven't given me much of a play. Nikos had tried to say please as nicely as he knew how, and they'd ignored him. Now he wanted to make a big splurge; to go over the top by way of their dead bodies, if you see what I mean."

"He was that kind of fighter," Chambrun said.

"I don't mind telling you, without too much personal vanity, the showing is sensational. Monica has arranged to stage it in really brilliant style; poor Rosey was all set to handle the publicity angles. If everything had gone smoothly, I think Nikos would have won his battle and I'd have been launched to—to the moon. Exclusivity; no mass production at least until the next showing. Lazar clothes worn by only a few society names, like Dodo Faraday, and by one or two big stars in the entertainment world. Everyone wanting to buy, only a few able to. By the time we came to my next showing, the whole fashion world would be drooling to get to me. This time, exclusivity; next time, the world."

"So?" Chambrun said.

"So now it takes on a whole new climate," Lazar said. "Nikos's murder will be front-page news in the morning. It will obscure the interest in what I have to show. Idiot women will be gossiping about Nikos, his women, his life. My things will be nothing in the background."

"You want to call off the showing?"

"I want your advice," Lazar said, "as Nikos's friend. You see I know what he has done for me in his will. I can afford to wait, now. I can come up with a new showing in six months, with all the outside sensationalism forgotten. I'll make it on my own merits. But—"

"Yes, Mr. Lazar?"

"Nikos so much wanted to win this battle with the fashion

writers and the rag-trade papers. We'd make it, you see, in a whirl of sensationalism that will really have nothing to do with my clothes. We'll fill all the fashion columns, but it will be because there is a murder involved and not because my designs are great. Should I go ahead for Nikos's sake, or should I use my own judgment now that I'm on my own?"

"Nikos would be pleased, I think, that you care about his wishes," Chambrun said. "He also cared about you as a creative talent, or he wouldn't have left you five years of security. I can't make a judgment about your business, Lazar, but I think I knew Nikos well enough to say that he'd leave it to you if he couldn't be here to run the show himself."

Lazar nodded slowly. "I've been trying to convince myself of that because I wanted to."

"But I would prefer it if you held back the announcement, publicly and privately, till late tomorrow afternoon—in time for Friday's morning papers. I don't want all the people connected with it taking off to the four corners until we've had every opportunity to get at the truth."

Lazar lifted his head. "The whole thing is unbelievable," he said. "Nikos—I loved him. A few hours ago I'd have said everyone who had dealings with him loved him. All *these* people, at least." He hesitated. "I'm worried about Jan. I understand she's among the missing. Your security people have been asking questions."

Chambrun's face went curiously blank.

"Poor Rosey was killed because she somehow hit on the truth about who switched Nikos's pills," Lazar went on. "Rosey was reasonably close to Nikos. But Jan was very close. For two years she has been the closest person to him, round the clock. He trusted her. He loved her, like a man and like a father. She must have been the repository for hundreds of secrets. Nikos was no fool, Chambrun. You know that. If there was someone who wanted him dead, it's a hundred to one Nikos would have caught wind of it. Jan is the person he might have talked to about it. Something Nikos discussed with Jan might suddenly light up the sky for her, and she'd become very dangerous to the killer."

"An interesting theory," Chambrun said, as though it was a brand-new idea. "It has been suggested, however, she might have killed Nikos herself to keep him from finding out about Faraday."

Lazar snorted. "Only an outsider would consider such a notion. You think Nikos didn't know about Mike?"

"I assume he didn't. From what Jan told Mark, she assumed he didn't."

"You're imagining Nikos as a cuckolded old idiot," Lazar said. He sounded angry. "He was a man who understood the facts of life. The girl had to have some sex, and he couldn't provide it. She was never missing when he needed her; he trusted her in every other area; so he closed his eyes to Faraday."

"He told you that?"

"Of course not. But I knew Nikos. He never missed a trick about anything. It had to be that way."

"It's possible," Chambrun said, his eyes hidden under their heavy lids.

"It's certain," Lazar said. "You've probably heard talk. Everyone's been jabbering upstairs. They say Jan was available to anyone who asked. That's not so."

"How do you know?"

"I asked," Lazar said, his mouth grim. "Oh, she has a great line about being a free spirit, and all that. But she's choosy. I must say I don't care for her choice of Faraday, but who can explain what turns on sexual electricity?"

I thought of Gallivan and Pappas, who had both implied

Jan had offered to play games with them. And then I remembered an odd contradiction. She'd talked about Gallivan once; how now, with Nikos dead, she'd have to get out her track shoes.

"Did Jan have many friends outside Nikos's own little family group?" I heard Chambrun asking.

Lazar shrugged. "For the last two years she's scarcely been away from Nikos's side for a minute. Between you and me, I don't know when she found the time to carry on an affair with Faraday. Wherever Nikos stayed, she had an adjoining bedroom. Her job was to check on him at regular intervals—he was deathly afraid of those heart attacks, poor devil. When he traveled, which was always by train or on the *Merina*, she was never away from him. She had no time for outside friends. But before she came to Nikos, well, I have no knowledge of that. She was only twenty. I know nothing about her family. She was a model for a while before she joined Nikos, working for Zach Chambers. He might know about her."

"He was her agent?"

"Yes."

"What about Chambers? What was his relationship with Nikos?"

Lazar's smile was weary. "Zach is an unhappy fellow," he said. "He's a queer, you know. He's getting along in years and he isn't as attractive to the young fry as he used to be. It's started him drinking pretty heavily. He's also a compulsive gambler, which keeps him constantly broke. But he's a genius at picking and schooling girls who can model. He gets along fine with girls, because he creates no problems for them outside his business dealings with them. He knows, instinctively, whether a girl can wear elegant clothes and not seem cheap. You saw Suzie Sands upstairs. That voice! I'd never in the world choose her to wear my designs, but Zach was right about her. On the runway, in the right clothes, she looks like a princess."

"You still haven't told me how Chambers got along with Nikos," Chambrun said.

"Nikos had respect for talent. Zach wasn't the kind of person Nikos would have for a friend, but Nikos respected him in a business way. Ever since Nikos became interested in fashion, Zach has provided models for him. Zach made a healthy package out of the deal. They only had one quarrel that I know of."

"Oh?"

"It was about Jan," Lazar said. "Zach thought she had the potential to be one of the great fashion models. She represented a gold mine to him. When Nikos picked her for his own private property, Zach was burned to a crisp. He made such a fuss he almost lost out with Nikos."

"But if Jan had friends before Nikos, Chambers might know about them?" Chambrun asked. "You see, if she's hiding out somewhere, she could have gone into her past for help."

"Zach could be helpful—if you can sober him up," Lazar said. "He was stoned to the gills the last I saw him."

The office door opened and Jerry Dodd came in. Lazar stood up.

"I'll need help," the designer said. "With Rosey gone, I don't quite know how to go about the business of releasing the word that my showing is canceled."

"Mark will help you in the morning," Chambrun said.

Jerry stood aside and watched Lazar leave. Then he joined us.

"No sign of the girl," he said.

"I want a crash search, Jerry," Chambrun said. "Maids are to go into every room they can with towels, whatever.

Where that doesn't work, I want a repair man to insist on being admitted—electrical short circuit, water leak, any excuse."

"There'll be some loud howls from a couple of dozen illicit Romeos," Jerry said.

"Let 'em howl. I want every room in the hotel covered."

"Right."

"I want doormen, Maggio's whole night crew, night watchmen, the whole staff alerted."

"Consider it done."

"How long will it take?"

"Couple of hours," Jerry said.

"Pressure it."

Jerry took off and Chambrun rose from his desk chair. "I've got a feeling we're too damned late," he said. "Our best hope is that phone call. If she got to some old friend's place and called from there—" He shrugged as though he didn't place much hope in the idea. "Let's have a go at Zach Chambers."

2

CHAMBERS HAD Room 1920, directly across the hall from Monica Strong's room. There was no answer when we knocked on his door. Chambrun produced a pass key and we went in.

I was almost knocked over by the sour, stale smell of liquor. All the lights in the room were blazing, and Zach was sprawled face down on his bed, out cold. I tried shaking him, and the only result was a low moan. Chambrun picked up the phone and called room service for hot coffee.

I went into the bathroom and soaked a towel in cold water. Somehow I got Zach rolled over on his back and went to work on him, slapping his face, trying the wet towel at the back of his neck. He moaned and groaned, but he showed no signs of coming to. After a bit the room service waiter arrived with coffee. Between us we pulled Zach up into a sitting position and got some coffee into his mouth. It was scalding hot.

His eyes rolled up into his head and he tried, feebly, to push us away.

"Get him up on his feet and walking," Chambrun said.

The waiter and I struggled with him. He was dead weight between us, his feet dragging. I kept slapping him and talking to him. He began to protest now, trying for words.

"Oh, please—for God sake!" I was able to distinguish.

We kept at it, getting coffee down him after each lap up and down the room. Finally his eyes focused on me.

"For God sake, go away!" he pleaded.

"When you come around enough to answer some questions, Zach, we'll let you go back to sleep."

"I'm sick!"

"So come in the bathroom and be sick," I said.

"What do you want? What in the name of God do you want?" He began to cry.

Chambrun slapped him so hard a red welt appeared on his flabby white cheek. "I want to ask you about Jan Morse, Chambers. We'll keep at you until you're ready to talk. You can save yourself a lot of discomfort if you'll listen and answer."

"I'll t-try," Zach stammered. "Only please let me sit down. The whole damn place is spinning around."

"If you go to sleep, I'll give you a real going-over, friend," I said.

"Look, man, I told you I'd try," Zach said.

The waiter and I eased him down into an armchair. His head lolled to one side. I slapped him.

"Please! Please just ask me and go away," Zach cried. Tears were rolling down his cheeks.

"Jan is missing," I said. "We're trying to find her. We need your help."

"Look for Faraday," he said. "Five to two, you'll find Jan

wherever Faraday is."

"Faraday is at police headquarters being questioned," Chambrun said. "Jan's not with him."

Zach's eyes tried to focus. "Faraday killed Rosey? Oh, that sonofabitch. Rosey was my friend. I loved her. I—"

"About Jan," Chambrun said. "Who were Jan's friends here in New York before she joined Nikos? Models she worked with. Boy friends."

"How would I know? How the hell would I know?"

"She was a model client of yours."

"Business," Zach wailed, "not social!"

"Think hard!" Chambrun said.

Zach rolled his head from side to side. "If you've got Faraday—he—he's your man. He was trying to find out about her. He—he asked me the same things. Who were her friends? He wanted to get something on her."

"What do you mean, get something on her?" Chambrun asked.

"He wanted her free of Nikos, don't you see?"

"No, I don't see."

"Mike wanted to get Jan away from Nikos. He—he couldn't just go to Nikos and say he was having a thing with Jan. Nikos would have clobbered him, man. So Mike was trying to find something in her past that would make Nikos get rid of her. Then Mike would have her to himself."

"What did he find?"

"Nothing—at least as far as I know. I didn't have anything to tell him. I wouldn't, even if I had. Faraday is a mean sonofabitch. I wouldn't spit on him if he was on fire." He took a deep swig of coffee. It seemed to be helping.

"All she had to do was walk out on Nikos if she wanted to belong to Faraday," I said.

Zach indulged in a sickly laugh. "You didn't just 'walk out' on Nikos, man. And anyway, I don't think Jan wanted to leave him."

Chambrun nodded toward the door. He'd had enough of Zach.

"Try and get sobered up," I said. "We may be back."

In the corridor Chambrun stood scowling, tugging at his lower lip. "Faraday," he said. "He is not the kind of man who lets his plans be sidetracked. We only have his word for it that he and Jan had a drink at some bar and then separated, he to go home, she to return here."

"We could do some checking at the local pubs," I said.

"There is one way a man like Faraday could have solved his lust problems," Chambrun said.

"Switching Nikos's pills?"

Chambrun nodded. "He could afford to wait for that plan to work. Miss Lewis was a smart woman. She probably knew he'd been playing games to get something on Jan so Nikos would dump her. She put it to him—and we know how violent his reactions can be."

"And Jan?"

"She guessed and told him to go peddle his paper. God help her." He glanced at his wrist watch. "Get Joe Cameron to take a quick skirmish around the neighborhood bars, Mark. I'll call Hardy at headquarters. It may give him a new line of questioning before Faraday's lawyer can spring him."

We started down the corridor just as the door to Jan's room, 1907, opened and Sergeant Jansen came out.

"Just starting out to look for you, Mr. Chambrun," he said. "I've called the Lieutenant and he's on his way back here."

"You've found some solid evidence?" Chambrun asked.

"This is a no-evidence case," Jansen said. "But we're pretty damn sure of one thing. The Lewis woman never went out the window in this room. Come on back in and I'll show you."

We followed him into 1907. One of the technicians was still there packing up his gear.

"Look over here," Jansen said, and led us to the still open window. The little piece of tweed from Rosey's smart suit was no longer attached to the air conditioner. Jansen pointed to the top of the air conditioner.

"The window was always kept closed," he said. "If you look at the top of the air conditioner, you can see three different accumulations of dust and dirt. Inside the window it's relatively clean. I assume the hotel maids dusted each day. There's some dust now, but the window's been open for several hours. Then you can see the area where the window came down on the metal box. Two little ridges of dirt—like a railroad track—the one on the outside thicker than the one on the inside. Then the portion of the conditioner which was outside the building is thickly coated with grime and soot."

"They all seem like logically differing accumulations," I said.

"But except for a few little smears around the little projection where the cloth was caught, none of the dust layers have been disturbed." Janson took a cigar out of his pocket and chewed on it without lighting it. "It's possible, if it was a suicide, that the Lewis girl could have taken a running swan dive out the window without touching the top of the air condtioner or the window frame on either side. It's possible but it would have been a circus trick. If she was killed and shoved out the window, the top of that air conditioner would show it. And let's forget the idea of a clean jump. We're supposed to think her suit caught on the air conditioner and a piece was ripped off it. So she did touch the top of the air conditioner and a piece was ripped off it. So she did touch the top of the air conditioner. Only she didn't. Dust and dirt undisturbed."

"Then this was a frame-up," Chambrun said.

"And a clumsy one," Jansen said. He turned away from the window, teeth clamped down hard on his unlit cigar. "We have a collection of fingerprints in the room, mostly Jan Morse's. There are some of Faraday's. There's another collection, but since they're mostly around electrical connections and bathroom fixtures, I'm guessing the maid. There are some others we haven't identified yet, but none of them near the window." Jansen turned back to stare at the window. "Someone in a hurry wanted us to believe the Lewis girl went from here. Well, she didn't. Now we've done some experting on the trajectory of the body's fall. It was found almost directly under this window, but depending on how it was thrown—or how she took off—she could have fallen from the next room to the north—Monica Strong's, Karados's bedroom to the south, or just possibly Gallivan's room, still further south."

"That would be stretching, wouldn't it—Gallivan's room?"

"Yeah," Jansen said. "But let me stretch, Mr. Chambrun. In Gallivan's room there is an air conditioner in one window, nothing in the other. That second window is interesting. The window sill, inside and out, has been wiped clean. Dust evenly removed from one side of the sill to the other, both inside and out. No fingerprints, no nothing."

"Proving?"

"That somebody cleaned the window sill," Jansen said. "Who? Well, Tim Gallivan heads the list, only because it's his room. But dozens of people milled in and out of all the rooms, especially his and Jan Morse's, connected as they were to Karados's. Nothing to really pin anything on anyone."

Chambrun nodded slowly. "A no-evidence case, as you said, Sergeant. We know Nikos died because someone played games with his pills. But no evidence as to who it was. We know Miss Lewis was thrown out a window in Gallivan's room, but no evidence as to who did it. An endless number of people had the opportunity to do both things, and most of them may have had a motive. Jan Morse undoubtedly has guessed at the truth. Because she's missing, she may actually have evidence. But she's missing."

"If she has evidence, forget about her," Jansen said. "The killer's had a couple of hours to deal with her."

Chambrun's narrowed eyes lifted. "Nikos checked into the Beaumont six days ago," he said. "He got a fresh prescription from Dr. Partridge for nitro pills that first day. The shift was made after that; today, yesterday, six days ago. Someone not present today for the showing and the party could have done it. But Miss Lewis was murdered while the party was going on. To the best of my knowledge only two people who attended the party have been allowed to leave the hotel—Faraday and Jan Morse herself. If Faraday isn't the villain of the piece, then Jan Morse is going to be found, alive or dead, somewhere in the hotel. We'll know in a little while."

"We know she called from outside," I said.

"On an outside line, not necessarily from outside the hotel," Chambrun said.

"It seems to me we should begin with Gallivan," Jansen said. "It was his room." He shook his head. "The hell of it is that photographer had a picture of whoever it was! You think his memory could be jogged?"

"I don't think he saw anything in that room except the two people he was shooting," I said. "He wouldn't have been aware of anything else until he developed the films. They're gone."

"No evidence again," Jansen said. "Well, let's pick up Gallivan. Even at a drunken binge a man is apt to notice who goes in and out of his room."

I felt as if some kind of time bomb was ticking away inside me, and I didn't know what time it was set to go off. There was the dark possibility that it had already exploded; that it was too late to do anything for Jan. I kept telling myself we still had a chance, and I was damned if I wanted to hang around listening to Jansen's no-evidence department, the exasperatingly slow, step-by-step approach to a blank wall. I took Chambrun aside.

"Can I go out on the town with Joe Cameron?" I asked him. "Two of us can cover more territory than one. And I know some of these small bars. Shelda and I go to some of them when we need to get away for a little. I have friends."

"Go," Chambrun said. I wasn't sure he'd really heard me. He seemed lost in a thick fog.

Joe Cameron and I started out together. It was agreed I'd take the crosstown streets, because that's where the places I knew were located—between the hotel and Shelda's apartment. Joe would take Madison and Lexington Avenues, a block or two in each direction.

I struck gold the very first joint I hit. It was a crummy little joint called *Mac's Place*, just down the block from the hotel. The owner, and usually the night bartender, was a jovial mick named Pat McNertney. He used to be a small-time heavyweight fighter, whose nose was crooked from poundings, and who sported a beautiful cauliflower ear. He used to buy Shelda and me a drink about once a month—after we'd bought about ten apiece. His place was almost empty and he looked glad to see me.

"Jack Daniels?" he asked me cheerfully.

"No time, Pat," I said. "I'm looking for someone who may have been in here a while back. Guy in a brown suit with a chocolate-colored turtle-neck shirt, and a girl in raspberry pink with a lot of blonde hair."

"Sure they were here," Pat said, polishing a glass. "A lot earlier. They were having at each other—cat and dog."

"Quarreling?"

"I'll tell the world," Pat said. "Guy shouting at the gal, and she talking low, but very tenselike."

"How long did they stay?"

"Three double vodkas for him, one root beer for her. Pretty soon the gal charged out and left him behind. That's when he ordered his third double."

"He didn't follow her?"

"Hell, no. He came over to the bar for his last drink. He was cooking over a hot flame, you know? Said all women were a pain in the you-know-what. I felt sorry for him, kind of. If he missed out with that pink lady, he missed out on a real package."

"You're sure he didn't follow her?"

"Look, Mark, the way she tore out of here she could've been in Hoboken by the time he finished that last drink." Pat poured me the Jack Daniels I'd refused. "What the hell's going on at your place? I see a lot of police cars."

"Woman went out a window from high up," I said.

"Thank God they always go to the fancy places to die," Pat said. "Anyone you knew?"

"Someone I liked real well," I said. I tossed off the drink, which I figured was less than an ounce and a half. The glass had a thick bottom. "If you see any sign of that raspberry kid again, give me a call. I need to find her, but bad."

"She won't be back here," Pat said. "She didn't enjoy herself."

It was a thin trail, but a trail. Jan had had plenty of time to get away from Faraday. If he'd stayed for a drink, he'd have had just about time to go home, change into his white silk karate outfit, get warned by his wife, and been ready to receive Chambrun, Hardy and me. There'd been no time for him to catch up with Jan, harm her, hide her, and get back to his Fifth Avenue mansion before we caught up with him.

I hightailed it back to the Beaumont and up to Chambrun's office. He wasn't alone. Hardy and Jansen were with him along with Tim Gallivan. Gallivan looked stunned.

"I've just been hearing the news that my room was used by someone as the place to do away with Rosey," he said to me. "God Almighty."

I relayed Pat McNertney's story. I couldn't tell what Chambrun made of it. His hooded eyelids were lowered.

"Let's get back to what must have happened in your room, Mr. Gallivan," Hardy said.

"I was in and out a lot—till toward the end," Gallivan said. He glanced at Chambrun. "Toward the end I came up with something tasty and—and I locked the door. I didn't come out till someone hammered on the door and said you were looking for me, Chambrun. Before that shank end I was mostly in Nikos's suite. In the beginning I was, in effect, the host. My job to circulate; make sure everybody was having a good time, which was Nikos's wish. Then—then the word came about Rosey, and I kept trying to keep people from starting a mass hysteria." Gallivan reached in his pocket for a cigarette. "I was shocked beyond belief myself, but I had to try to keep things calm. I had to think of Lazar's showing on Friday. That was Nikos's last wish. Maxie's line should go over with a bang. I've still got to get that show on the road, no matter what else."

Chambrun's eyelids lifted. "It's been called off," he said.

"You can't do that!" Gallivan said. "Nikos worked for months to set it up." He looked at Hardy, his eyes suddenly blazing. "How can it possibly interfere with your investigation, Lieutenant? Hell, it will keep the people you're interested in all here under one roof."

"I didn't call it off," Hardy said.

"Lazar's wish," Chambrun said.

"The stupid bastard! He can't do that to Nikos!" Gallivan said. "Look, I'm sorry, gents, but I've got to talk to Max. He can't do this."

Chambrun picked up the house phone on his desk and asked for Lazar's room. Then, quietly: "Would you mind coming down to my office, Mr. Lazar?"

"Does Monica know?" Gallivan asked. "She's put in months of work on this."

"About your room," Hardy said. He wasn't concerned with fashion shows. "You're positive you didn't see Miss Lewis go into your room?"

"Sonofabitch suddenly thinks he's a big shot now that Nikos is gone," Gallivan said.

"Miss Lewis was pitched out that window," Hardy said, "and then the killer took time to clean away all traces. Maybe a piece of her tweed suit was torn off as she went out. Maybe he deliberately tore off a piece of it before he heaved her out the window. It makes an interesting point, Mr. Gallivan. Why would he want to make us think it happened in Miss Morse's room? It was risky to go through the motions of setting up that fake."

"How the hell do I know why?" Gallivan said. He was clearly thinking about Lazar.

"Cleaning off the window still in your room makes sense," Hardy said. "He had to make sure he wouldn't leave any fingerprints. But why, then, the fake-off in Miss Morse's room? What difference would it make to him what room it happened in, if he didn't leave evidence behind him? It would work just as well for you to be suspected as Miss Morse, wouldn't it?"

"Unless," Chambrun said, in a faraway voice.

"Unless what?" Gallivan said.

"Unless it was you, Gallivan," Chambrun said. "You might try to point somewhere else."

"Oh, for God sake come off it," Gallivan said in a disgusted voice. "You bastards haven't got a single lead to this mess. Don't try to fake out on me, chums. Hell, Rosey was my very good friend. Why should I—"

"That's par for the course," Hardy said. "Everyone was Rosey's 'very good friend'—except someone wasn't. Rosey went to a very good friend—in your room, Gallivan—and said, 'You shifted Nikos's pills,' and the very good friend clobbered her, threw her out the window, and then tried to make it look as though it had happened somewhere else. Why, unless as Chambrun suggests, it was you?"

Gallivan grinned his Irish grin. "Well, if I did, it didn't work. So what's new, Lieutenant?" He held out his hands. "You want to match my fingerprints with some you've found around? Help yourself. Couldn't we be a little less absurd? Nikos was my closest friend, my brother, my benefactor. I would have died myself rather than let him be knocked off. Rosey knew that. Whoever she suspected, you can bet your life on it it wasn't me. And if she had suspected me, I'd have laughed at her, taken her by the hand, bought her a drink, and told her to wise up." He shook his head as though Hardy was a stubborn child. "The people who were double-crossing Nikos were Jan and Faraday. Faraday, with his temper, is the kind of guy who would kill someone and then figure out afterwards what to do about it."

"Like framing his girl?" Chambrun asked.

"A little while ago you had Jan pegged as the killer," I said.

"I still think she may be. She, or Faraday, or both together."

"Carefully pointing a finger at themselves?" Chambrun asked.

Gallivan's relaxed grin widened. "Since you were bound to discover it was a fake, it would actually point away from them, wouldn't it? Not too stupid, when you stop to think."

The office door opened and Max Lazar came in. Gallivan's grin vanished.

"What's this about your calling off the showing, Maxie?" he asked.

Lazar looked at the two cops, puzzled. "Is there some reason why—"

"You're damn right there's a reason why," Gallivan said, his voice rising. "You know what Nikos wanted. You know how carefully he planned it. What the hell's the reason for calling it off?"

"Personal reasons, Tim. The show will be buried under murder and scandal. No one will pay the slightest attention to my designs. They'll be lost in the headlines. Nikos wouldn't want that to happen. So I wait—until the next time around."

"I won't have it!" Gallivan said. "Nikos's wishes are going to be carried out, down to the last dotting of an 'i' and the crossing of a 't.' That show is going on, Max, come hell or high water."

There was surprising strength in Lazar's dark face. "I'm sorry, Tim, but I've made up my mind. I have to think of myself. And I'm thinking of Nikos, too. He wouldn't have wanted me to lose out."

"You'll go through with it, Max, or you'll wish to God you'd never been born."

"I take it, Gallivan, you're executor of Nikos's will," Chambrun said quietly. "Do you have some special authority to alter its provisions? Mr. Lazar has full control of his inheritance, hasn't he?"

Gallivan's voice was unsteady. "Yes. Unfortunately I can't do anything about that." He swung around at Lazar. "It's taken money to build you up, Maxie. It's taken connections to get to the right people to wear your clothes at the right time and at the right places. I do have access to those connections. I do count the important buyers in the high-fashion field among my friends—and Nikos's. I can snow you under forever, Maxie, if I choose. And I choose, if you don't go through with this showing."

"Either I have something to offer or I don't," Lazar said. "If I can be wiped out by your pulling strings with your friends, I'd better find it out now and turn to something that isn't based on such a whimsical foundation."

Gallivan changed his tack. His manner became smooth as velvet. "Look, Maxie, I'm your friend," he said. "You know that. I've handled all Nikos's business details as they relate to you. I encouraged him to go all-out for you. You know that. I think you owe it to him and to me to go through with what he planned for you."

"I don't see why it's so important to you," Lazar said. "It's my judgment, and Mr. Chambrun, who was also Nikos's friend, agrees with me, that it would be a personal disaster to go ahead with the showing in the face of all this trouble."

"Damn Mr. Chambrun!" Gallivan exploded. "You want me to play rough, Maxie, I will. I promise you."

It was a strange kind of argument. Hardy and Jansen, the two cops, concerned with a multiple killing and a missing key witness, seemed to have been taken back by the sheer violence of Gallivan's attack. Gallivan, who should have been worrying about the fact that a crime had probably been committed in his room and that he was certainly on the prime list of suspects, seemed to have forgotten everything except his outrage at Lazar's decision. It didn't make sense to me. The showing was Lazar's ball game to win or lose.

Gallivan turned to Hardy. "I don't like to drop out of your little game of pin the tail on the donkey, Lieutenant, but I've got to try to make this idiot make sense." He spun back at Lazar. "Have you talked to Monica?"

Lazar shook his head. "There isn't any reason to talk to anyone, Tim. It's my decision to make, and I've made it."

"Monica Strong knows more about this field than all of us put together," Gallivan said. "Do me the favor of talking to her before you do anything final."

"Well, yes, I'll talk to her," Lazar said. "I have to tell her the showing is off."

"Will you listen to her?"

"Sure, I'll listen." Lazar looked at me. "Would you come along with me, Haskell? Monica may have some very sound advice about who the press people are who should be told at once."

I very much didn't want to go. The only thing that really concerned me at the moment was Jan. If Jerry Dodd or anyone else came up with any kind of a lead, I wanted to be on deck to help. Finding her seemed to be the most important thing on the agenda.

"Go along with Mr. Lazar, Mark," Chambrun said.

I looked at him reproachfully. His stony face told me nothing.

"I'll let you know if there's any news," he said.

"Let's go," Gallivan said. "I hope Monica can talk some sense into you, Maxie."

"I'm sorry, Gallivan, but I'm not through with you," Hardy said.

"Will you knock off this nonsense!" Gallivan almost shouted at him. "I don't know anything about your windows and your frame-ups. If I knew anything that would help you, I'd tell you, but I don't. This business of Maxie's is vitally important to me. I've got to go with him to Monica."

"When I'm through with you," Hardy said, unbudging.

"God-damned idiots!" Gallivan said, his face dark with anger.

"You and Lazar run along, Mark," Chambrun said.

I knew that ultra-quiet tone of voice of Chambrun's. Something was cooking with him.

Lazar and I went to the outer office together. I suggested he call Monica Strong to make sure where she was. He found her on her room phone. She told him she'd meet us in the Trapeze in about ten minutes.

We walked down into the lobby together and up the short flight of stairs to the Trapeze. The crowed had thinned out a little there and Mr. Del Greco had no trouble finding us a table. We each ordered a drink. Lazar's dark young face looked almost painfully exhausted.

"It's a hard choice to make, you know, but it's a hell of a lot harder for me than for Tim. I've put in months of design work." He shook his head. "He makes it sound as though it was costing him something personally."

"Was he an investor?" I asked.

"Nikos was the only angel," Lazar said. "The money that's been spent so far means absolutely nothing to Nikos's estate. Peanuts that can be written off as a business expense against taxes." The waiter brought his drink, but he just toyed with it. "It's hard to believe he could be so violent over a change of plans that will cost him nothing." He looked at me and gave me a weary little smile. "You're not with me. You're still concerned about Jan?"

"No trace of her," I said. "We're going over the hotel inch by inch, from roof to basement. Frankly, I'm not hopeful."

"Zach had nothing to offer?"

"No help as far as finding her is concerned."

"Ask Monica when she comes," Lazar said. "You know, Monica was in Jan's position for about ten or twelve years—Nikos's girl, his confidante. She may have been a great deal more to Nikos than Jan is. She was with him long before he had his first heart attack. She was his woman, his hostess, the caretaker of his pleasures. Not unreasonably, she resents Jan. But she might know special routines that Jan might follow in trouble."

He didn't go on because Monica appeared in the doorway. She'd changed from her party dress of the afternoon into a deceptively simple black knitted thing that did a great deal for her still gorgeous figure. We stood up as she came across the room to our table. As she sat down between us, I was aware of an elusive perfume.

"What's up?" she asked.

"I've decided not to go ahead with the showing," Lazar said.

She drew a deep breath and let it out in a long sigh. She looked at me. "I wonder if I might have a vodka and tonic?" she asked. She opened her little gold mesh bag and took out a cigarette. I held my lighter for her and then signaled to the waiter and ordered her drink. "I've been thinking you might come to that, Max," she said. "Well, that's a lot of work gone down the drain. It was going to be a lovely party."

"You think I'm wrong?" Lazar asked. "Tim is outraged by it. He thinks I owe it to Nikos to go ahead. He threatens to have the buyers and the press down on my back for the rest of my life."

She smiled a thin little smile. "Tim is not Nikos," she said. "If Nikos threatened you, you could be sure he could make it stick. Tim is the heir apparent, but he isn't Nikos. We've all got to learn to make our own decisions now. New world, Max, for all of us."

"Do you feel I owe it to Nikos to go ahead?"

She didn't answer at once. The waiter brought her drink and she turned it round and round in her slim fingers. "Sentiment is a commodity that's pretty well disappeared from the world these days," she said. "Nikos was taking a huge delight in putting you over at this time, Max. He would have done it. It might still happen, but without him, you can't be certain. Nikos could afford to be a sentimentalist. But can you? Practically, I think you're right in waiting. I'm sorry about it. It would have been a fine sendoff for me in a world without Nikos. But for you I think the decision is correct."

"You think it's sentiment that has Tim so upset?"

She laughed outright. "Tim is about as sentimental as an armor-plated tank," she said. "No, I think our Tim has other problems. The king is dead, long live the king—only the subjects will suddenly scatter. He gives an order to you, Max, and you disobey it. That's his first taste of what it's going to be like. An empire is already slipping through his fingers. Did you ask his advice before you decided?"

"No," Max said.

"That's how it's going to be," Monica said, "from everyone. You wouldn't have dreamed of making a move on your own without consulting Nikos, would you? Tim imagined it would be like that for him. In just a few hours the whole thing is coming apart at the seams for him." She smiled, and it had a Cheshire cat quality.

"You're not fond of Gallivan, are you?" I said.

She turned to give me a very direct look. "Is it that obvious? Oh, you can't trust me, Haskell. I'm a vindictive, bitchy gal. Remember, I'm the deposed queen. Tim treated me like royalty for ten years. All I had to do was raise an eyebrow and I got what I was thinking about. I liked him in those days, even trusted him. He was Nikos's right arm. It seemed to me he had a genius for anticipating everything Nikos wanted. His financial and legal judgments were invariably right. He was a perfect gentleman, with courtesy and humor about everything he did. And then Nikos had his heart attack and I was given my walking papers. Now I was on the outside, and my every wish was no longer law to Tim. I began to see another side of him that had been hidden from me up to then."

"He wasn't all the things you'd thought he was?"

A thin frown creased her forehead. "I'm not sure. I mean, I'm not sure he didn't change at that point. After Nikos's heart attack. He knew, you see, that Nikos was going to die in the foreseeable future. He knew that he was the prime beneficiary—the Prince of Wales. He knew that just around the next corner he'd come into the money and the power. I became aware that he made little jokes about Nikos behind his back. I could see him setting up things for himself, so they'd be ready when his big moment came. I became aware, on the outside, for the first time that he was a woman chaser to end all women chasers. He had the nerve to make passes at me. I was no longer in a protected position. He indulged in that pastime to an extent that would have outraged Nikos. I even think he imagines that he'll inherit Jan. I doubt if he will, though."

"You know she's turned up missing?" Max said.

"Jan?"

I told her how it was, and she listened, staring down into her pale drink with its twist of lemon.

"You seem to have learned a good deal about Nikos's world, Haskell," she said when I'd finished, not looking at me. "I'm not fond of Jan. Why pretend? The old shoe replaced by the new; middle age outrun by youth. Don't misunderstand. Jan didn't connive to take my place. I—I ceased to be of that kind if importance to Nikos."

"That's hard to believe," I said.

"Marriage was never in the scheme of things for Nikos," she said, her eyes still averted. "But I was his wife, in every true meaning of such a relationship. I loved him as a person; I loved his power; I loved having people know that I belonged to him. And then it happened." She took a tiny sip of her drink. "He had his heart attack, and fear came into his fearless life. Oh, my God, how he didn't want to die! Our—our relationship changed. 'You'll just become a housekeeper and a body servant,' he told me. 'You still can have a life. And I couldn't bear to have you around me, Monica. It would be a constant reminder of what I've lost.' And so—that was that. And then he got himself a toy—Jan—that he could look at and dream about. Of course I resent her. I would have stayed with Nikos to the very end, if only he'd let me." Then she looked straight at me for the first time. "She was good to Nikos; genuinely fond of him, I think. But there was Mike Faraday, and God knows who else. I've resented that. But I don't believe for an instant that she'd have done Nikos a harm. Kill him? Never. And if she had any idea who could have done it, I believe she'd fight for justice for Nikos. So—she may well be in very bad trouble."

"Haskell thought you might have ideas," Max said. "Where she might go to hide, or for help."

Monica's beautiful forehead was creased with a frown. "If—if something had happened in the old days, and I'd found myself in danger," she said slowly, "the first place I'd head for would be the *Merina*. Old Captain Pappas—and young George, who's taken over—would protect anyone who belonged to Nikos with their lives."

"Dodo Faraday called them Greek pirates," I said.

"The *Merina* was home base to me," Monica said. "It probably would be to Jan."

"Only she isn't there," I said. "Captain Pappas was here a while ago to see Gallivan. He called the yacht in my presence to see if Jan had shown up there. She hadn't."

She looked past me into some distant place. "It's hard to realize, but I suppose Tim is now the owner of the *Merina*." She shook herself free of that thought. "There were times in Nikos's life when he played really dangerous games," she said. "There was, for example, a head-on collision with the Mafia over a drug-smuggling thing that involved one of the crew members of the *Merina*. In those days, before the heart attack, Nikos was afraid of nothing for himself. But he was afraid for me. He was afraid someone might try to get at him through me. I had standing instructions. If he wasn't around and I had any reason to be afraid about anything, I was to go straight to Captain Pappas and stay put. That was the old Captain Pappas, who died about eighteen months ago. The *Merina's* men have arms—machine guns, rifles, depth charges. The crew could hold off a good-sized naval vessel if they had to."

"You'd have trusted the crew, then?" I said.

"With my life," she said. "I imagine Jan had the same kind of instructions."

"You think she might still go there?"

"If she can make it," Monica said.

"Why shouldn't she be able to make it?"

"Because there are plenty of other people who know that's where she'd probably go to be safe."

"Where is the yacht anchored?" I asked.

"Nikos leases a mooring space just off Seventy-third Street in the Hudson," Monica said. "I don't know why I should be helping you, Haskell. Do you have something you can write on? I'll show you how to make the shore-to-ship phone call.

It's an unlisted number."

I excused myself and went over to the bar, where I got Eddie to give me a phone. I vaguely remembered a small boat basin just off the beginnings of Riverside Drive. As I recalled it, there were mostly small outboards and family cabin cruisers, nothing large. But there had been a spell when the great sea-going Onassis yacht had been anchored there. As I remembered it, the approaches to the dock side were wide-open. You couldn't get to the water's edge to a small boat to take you out to the yacht without being easily spotted. If, as Monica suggested, somebody might be waiting there to keep Jan from getting to the *Merina*, there was no way she could manage it without being seen. It occurred to me that Captain Pappas could put some of his men ashore to watch for Jan. If it wasn't already too late, they could see to it that she made the yacht.

I dialed the number Monica had given me and promptly came up with an operator who gave me the "temporarily out of order" routine. Vaguely disturbed, I started back to the table.

We had company. It was the gorgeous Julie Christie model. She looked unhappy as I joined them. Monica introduced her as "Red Parsons, one of Zach's very best."

"I don't mean to be rude," the girl said to Monica, "but I did want to talk to you and Mr. Lazar in private, Miss Strong."

"If it's about the showing, Red, Mr. Haskell will be handling the promotion aspects now that Rosey's gone."

The girl's make-up was artistically applied, but I could see that she was unnaturally pale underneath it.

"It's about Miss Lewis I wanted to tell you," the girl said.

I pulled an extra chair up to the table and she sat down. Her hands were clasped so tightly together the knuckles showed white.

"What about her, Red?" Monica asked.

"It may be nothing at all," the Julie Christie girl said, "but I—I've been worried sick about it." She looked nervously at Max. "I was just coming to the party. I was very late because I'd been having a drink in the Trapeze with a photographer from *Vogue* who wants me for a sitting next week. I had on a new dress. I got on an elevator down in the lobby here and started up. It stopped at the second floor and Miss Lewis came in. She waved to someone I think was you, Mr. Haskell."

That had to be when she'd announced she was "a big girl" and started back to the party after her visit with Chambrun.

"We said hello," the model said, "and then I saw she was looking at me—her eyes kind of popping, if you know what I mean."

" 'Where did you get that dress, Red?' she asked me."

"I told her a friend gave it to me.

" 'What friend?' she wanted to know.

"Well, I was a little embarrassed to tell her, because she might think—well, she might think I was dishing out for favors. But she insisted on my telling her. When we got out of the elevator on the nineteenth floor, she wouldn't let me go to the party. Just insisted on knowing where I got the dress. So I told her. She was suddenly so mad it scared me."

"So where did you get the dress?" Monica asked.

"Bernie Dreyfus gave it to me," Red said. "I'm going to model a new line for them later this week. The dress was one of the items. I'd said how great I thought it was and he said go ahead and take it, as a gift from him. Bernie is something of a lech, but he's good-hearted. 'Only don't wear it till after Friday in public,' he said. Well, I couldn't see what harm it would do, and it was the smartest thing I had, so I decided to wear it to the party for Nikos, which really wasn't public, if you see what I mean. But Miss Lewis was burning. 'Do you know what you've got on, Red?' she said. 'That's one of the new Lazar designs that nobody has seen or bought. How did Bernie Dreyfus get it?' Well, of course I couldn't tell her because I didn't know."

Monica turned to me, and her face had turned strangely hard. "The Dreyfus Brothers are the biggest manufacturers of high-style fashion in cheap copies in the world," she said. "Once the Dreyfus Brothers copy a designer's line, every stenographer and suburban housewife in the country will be wearing them. No real fashion personality would be seen dead in them."

"It's not possible," Max said, his voice harsh.

"Of course I wouldn't know, Mr. Lazar," Red said, "because I haven't seen all your things. But Miss Lewis was certain. She kept saying, 'Every seam, the cut of the material, right down to the tiny buttonhole in the lapel. It's a perfect copy!' And she grabbed me and told me I was to go to my room and take it off. She didn't want you to see it, Mr. Lazar, until she did—'a little investigating,' she said. And then she said, 'That slimy bastard!' and she left me there with my mouth hanging open and went back to the party."

"Morrie Stein!" Lazar said. "He took advance photographs of some of the girls modeling a half dozen things so there'd be photographs for the press the minute the show was over. If he—" He stood up so abruptly his chair went over backward.

Monica reached out a hand to stop him. "Wait till you see the dress, Max," she said. "There were just three or four of us who have seen the line—beside the models who wore them. Morrie, who took the photographs; Rosey, who was going to write about them; I, who was going to stage the showing; and Tim Gallivan. And, of course, Nikos. That was absolutely all. If the copy is exact, it had to be done from a photograph."

Her smile was bitter. "One of us has sold you out, Max. Rosey guessed who, and died for it. Nikos is gone. That leaves Tim, and Morrie, and me. Take your choice."

The Julie Christie girl lifted a hand to her tightly drawn mouth. "Oh, Lord, do you suppose my wearing that dress is what made someone kill Miss Lewis?"

Monica's voice seemed to come from far away. "If Nikos had lived to know that someone had sold you out, Max, we'd have had a sample of the real wrath of God."

Max Lazar had the model by the arm and literally pulled her up out of her chair. "I want to see that dress," he said.

"Well, sure, Mr. Lazar. It's in my room upstairs."

"We go—now," Max said.

Monica watched them go and then she finished her drink and put the glass down hard on the table. "So now we know why Nikos and Rosey are gone," she said.

"I don't get it," I said. "Selling pictures of Lazar's designs was that important?"

"With Nikos alive?" She laughed. "I've pointed out to you there are just three of us who had access to those pictures—Tim, me, and Morrie. Morrie has a dark room assistant who could have developed the film and printed any number of sets of the photographs."

"What was supposed to happen?"

Monica shrugged. "Friday, Max's showing takes place. There would be a big publicity hoop-la. Saturday morning the cheap copies would appear in all the Dreyfus outlets—New York, Chicago, Dallas, Los Angeles. By Saturday night thousands of women all over the country would be wearing those cheap copies. Max's line would be dead as far as the real fashion trade is concerned."

"Why would anyone sell out?" I asked. "Would these Dreyfus people pay so much for an advance look at the designs?"

"Oh, they'd pay plenty," Monica said. "Without a leak it would take time, probably some weeks, for them to buy originals, plan how to make the cheap copies, and get them on the market. To come out with them, simultaneously with Max's showing, would make them a small fortune. They'd pay!"

"But whoever sold out is bound to be caught," I said, "even with Nikos dead. They'd know that in advance."

"Legally no crime has been committed," Monica said. "Nikos was the risk; his anger, his certain punishment."

"Too big a risk for you or Tim Gallivan to run," I said. "Dreyfus couldn't have paid enough to make it worth while for either of you. You didn't need that kind of money. Certainly Gallivan didn't need it. Either one of you could go to Nikos for twice the amount if you'd needed it—however much it was."

She stared down at her empty glass. "I can't think of any reason—I can't even invent one—why I might want to risk a sellout. Tim, either."

"I think you better come up with me to Chambrun's office," I said. "You can explain this all to him better than I can."

She offered no objection. She seemed almost lost in some kind of intense concentration. We took an elevator to the second floor and went directly to the Great Man's office. He was alone. Hardy and Gallivan were gone.

"I think we've come up with some kind of a motive," I said.

Monica, in a flat, unemotional voice, told him Red Parson's story about the dress, Rosey Lewis's outrage when she saw it. Chambrun listened, his eyes narrowed slits.

"I can invent a reason why you or Gallivan might have sold out, Miss Strong," he said. "If Dreyfus had something on you, something he could take to Nikos that would strike you out of Nikos's life, his will, he wouldn't have had to pay a cent for your services. You'd have to come through with photographs of the Lazar line or you were dead with Nikos. You'd do it, knowing that if you couldn't solve the problem before Friday, Nikos would have to go. A dead Nikos couldn't change his will."

Monica stared at him, her expression blank. "But I couldn't count on a heart attack," she said.

"That was a hope," he said. "If it didn't work, you'd have tried something else—something I once called Plan B." He reached for the house phone on his desk and asked for Mrs. Kiley. He switched on the conference box on his desk so we could all hear. "Please find a number for Bernard Dreyfus—home, at this hour. Call him for me."

"Yes, Mr. Chambrun."

"After that, Mrs. Kiley, any phone calls that come in for Timothy Gallivan, Miss Monica Strong, or Morris Stein are to be conferenced in on this line."

"Yes, sir."

Chambrun put down his phone. "Dreyfus will try to get in touch with his pigeon as soon as I'm through talking to him. Save us guessing," he said.

We sat in silence for a moment or two and then the phone rang.

"I have Mr. Dreyfus for you," Mrs. Kiley said.

Chambrun's voice was oil smooth as he said: "Hello, Mr. Dreyfus."

Dreyfus's voice was angry. "You know what time it is, Chambrun? One o'clock in the morning. You out of your cotton-picking mind?"

"I haven't seen you since your company held its sales dinner here last fall," Chambrun said.

"You trying to sell me another banquet at one o'clock in

the morning? You must be stewed!" Dreyfus said.

"I thought you'd be interested to know that the Max Lazar showing has been called off," Chambrun said.

We could hear a sharp intake of breath and then a kind of forced chuckle. "Why should that interest me?"

"Because of the new line you're about to launch," Chambrun said.

"What new line?" Dreyfus asked.

"The Lazar copies," Chambrun said. "If the originals are never shown, I thought you'd be in a little trouble. Worth waking you at one A.M., I thought."

"Somebody's given you a bum steer," Dreyfus said. "But thanks anyway. Ask me a favor sometime. I owe you."

His phone clicked off and Chambrun put down his receiver. He leaned back in his chair and lit one of his flat, Egyptian cigarettes. His bright eyes were fixed on Monica, who seemed to be in a kind of trance.

I don't suppose it was thirty seconds before the phone rang. Chambrun answered.

"There's a call for Miss Strong, Mr. Chambrun," Mrs. Kiley said. "Her room phone doesn't answer."

"She's here," Chambrun said. He held out the receiver to Monica. She moved like an automaton to take it. I felt the inside of my mouth go dry.

"Hello," Monica said.

"Hi, baby," Dreyfus's voice said. "Bernie Dreyfus here. Sorry to wake you this time of night."

"I wasn't asleep."

"Someone just called me to tell me Lazar's called off his Friday showing."

"That's true."

"Why?"

"He feels the sensationalism that will grow up because of

Nikos's murder would be too damaging."

"Murder!" Dreyfus's voice rose. "I thought it was a heart attack."

"It was murder."

"God Almighty." There was a pause and then Dreyfus said, "That crazy bastard!"

"Rosey Lewis, too," Monica said. "Why did you call me, Mr. Dreyfus?"

"Oh, that," Dreyfus said. "I thought maybe you could use your influence to get Lazar to change his mind. And if you couldn't—"

"Yes?"

"Well, I guess it's no secret we've got hold of the line ahead of time. You got a show ready to stage. If you aren't going to do it for Lazar, I thought you might move the whole package over and do it for Dreyfus Brothers. Make it worth your while."

"I'm sorry, Mr. Dreyfus. I don't think I could do that."

"Well, nothing lost by asking," Dreyfus said. "Look, baby, save me a dime by having the operator there transfer me to Tim Gallivan, will you?"

Monica glanced at Chambrun, who nodded. Monica jiggled the receiver and Mrs. Kiley's voice came through. "Yes, please?"

"Will you transfer this to Mr. Gallivan in nineteen hundred one?"

We could hear the phone ringing, and then Gallivan's voice, hoarse and tired, came through the conference box.

"Gallivan here."

"Okay, wise guy, so what's cooking?" Bernie Dreyfus asked.

"Oh, it's you, Bernie."

"It's me, dad. What's this about Lazar calling off his

show?"

"Where did you hear that?"

"Never mind where I heard it. It better not be so, dad."

"It's nothing to worry about," Gallivan said. "Monica's talking him out of it now."

"Like hell she is," Dreyfus said. "I just talked to her and she isn't talking him out of anything."

"Then I will," Gallivan said. "You can count on it, Bernie."

"I better count on it, dad," Dreyfus said. "I hear rumors that tell me I could make you pretty bad trouble if I can't count on you."

"Count on it," Gallivan said angrily, "and for God's sake stop blabbing over this switchboard telephone. I'll go talk to Max now."

"You better persuade him nice," Dreyfus said. "I got too much at stake here, dad. Call me when you know for sure—no matter what time it is."

"I will, Bernie. Keep your shirt on."

Chambrun shut off the phone.

"So it *is* Tim," Monica said in a whisper.

"It's always been Tim," Chambrun said. "Evidence we can hold him on? Not one shred. Dreyfus may have the answer for us. I'm going to see him now. I may be able to scare him into talking. I'd be scared if two people were already dead because of what I knew. I'll have Jerry cover Lazar to be sure nothing happens to him." He stood up. "Thank you for your help, Miss Strong." His smile was faint. "You had me going for a minute when Dreyfus asked for you."

"About Jan," I said.

"You've tried the *Merina?*" Chambrun asked.

"Ship-to-shore phone is on the blink," I said. "Monica's sure that's where she'd go."

"Why don't you take a run over to the West Side,"

Chambrun said. "It's safe enough. Gallivan's here and he'll be busy with Lazar."

"You can count on Captain Pappas," Monica said.

"It's my experience, Miss Strong, that the only person I can really count on is myself," Chambrun said.

"Thanks," I said.

He smiled at me. "You are part of me, Mark—you, and Ruysdale, and Jerry, and one or two others. Without you I wouldn't be me." His face darkened. "As things stand now, Gallivan can pack his bags and walk out of here. We've got nothing to hold him on. Dreyfus is our best bet."

A pale moon was fading slowly over the Palisades. My taxi took me within about fifty yards of the river's edge. Dozens of small boats bobbed on the water's choppy surface. Out in the center of the river I could see the long, graceful bulk of the *Merina,* lights in several cabin windows. The problem was to get out to her.

There was a little white-painted shed near the shore line, and I saw that there was a light in the window. It turned out to be the office of a night watchman who wasn't inclined to be helpful. He was an old gent, with a couple of days' growth of grizzled beard on his face.

"I can't take you out to the yacht without orders from Captain Pappas," he said. "How do I know you got any business out there?"

I showed him the slip of paper I had with the telephone number on it. "Does this check out with the number you've got?"

He scowled at it. "Maybe," he said.

"The yacht's phone is out of order," I said. "Try for yourself. If it's been fixed since I tried, tell Captain Pappas it's Mark Haskell. He'll send in a small boat for me."

Grudgingly the old man tried the phone on the table beside his coffeepot. I could hear the operator's voice telling him "temporarily out of order."

"I've got ten bucks that says you're too old to row me out to the yacht," I said.

The old man gave me a sour smile. "I'll take the bet," he said.

I got in the back of his dinghy and he started to row me out to the *Merina*. The Jersey shore was a dark mass, with almost no lights visible. The old man rowed slowly, methodically.

"We're going to miss Mr. Karados," he said. "Nice guy. Generous spender. One time when I was sick, before I came under Medicare, he paid all my hospital bills. They don't come like him often. Most of the guys who own the big boats are too snotty to know you're alive."

There was a gangway down the side of the yacht, and the old man eased us skillfully alongside. I gave him his ten-dollar bill. Someone with a thick accent hailed us from the deck.

"Someone to see Captain Pappas," the old man called up.

Then I heard a voice that gave me the biggest boost of the evening.

"Mark! I thought you'd never come," Jan called down to me from the deck.

I scrambled up the gangway and met her on the deck. She was still wearing the raspberry dress.

I saw the dark figure of the sailor who'd hailed us, evidently on his way to call Pappas.

"You're all right?" I asked Jan. She was standing close to me, and I put my hands on her arms. She smelled like flowers.

"Of course I'm all right," she said. "But you didn't come, and the phone was out of order, and George thought I should stay here until we had word from you."

"George?"

"Captain Pappas." She came even closer. "What happened when you faced Tim with it?"

"Faced him with what?"

"The message I sent you."

"What message? Let's start over from the beginning."

"The message I sent you by Captain Pappas," she said, her eyes widening. "What I knew about Tim."

"Pappas didn't deliver any message from you," I said. "I saw him at the Beaumont. He didn't bring any message."

Her fingernails bit into the flesh of my arms. "Oh, my God!" she said. She drew me along the deck toward a canvas-covered lounging area at the stern of the boat.

"Who did George see at the Beaumont?" she asked.

"Gallivan. I set them up with an office where they could talk. He never said anything about a message from you. He said he hadn't seen you. He called the yacht while I was with him and asked if you were here. They told him you weren't."

"He couldn't have called the *Merina*," she said. "The phone is out of order. It went out just after I called to ask how you and Miss Ruysdale were. Did you know I'd called?"

"Yes."

"Right after that the phone went out," Jan said. "I told George what I knew and he agreed to go ashore and tell you and Mr. Chambrun. You mean, like he never did?"

"He never did." I was holding her close to me and we spoke in whispers. "What do you know, Jan?"

"About Tim," she said. "Oh, it goes back some six months. I did the wrong thing then, I guess. But sometimes Nikos seemed so—so sort of square, if you see what I mean."

"What was he square about?"

"Oh, like his ideas about sex. And he would never forgive anyone for anything, no matter how good an excuse you might have for displeasing him. 'An old elephant,' Tim called him. 'Never forgets and never forgives.' "

"So?"

"There was a party like I said, six months ago. It was given by one of the big buyers for a West Coast store. There were designers, and fashion writers, and models—everyone who was anybody in the fashion world. I went with Rosey Lewis and Tim. It was kind of wild and gay. Among the people there was Bernard Dreyfus, one of the Dreyfus brothers. They are big manufacturers of copies of the top designers' stuff."

"I know about him," I said.

"Nikos hated him," Jan said. "It seems that back in World War Two the Dreyfus Brothers were collaborators with the Nazis. I guess you know from Mr. Chambrun that Nikos was on the other side. I remember thinking if Nikos knew I'd even said hello to Bernard Dreyfus, he might kick me out, bag and baggage. Well, at that party there was a man named Conrad Schwartzkopf. He was a big West German banker and a former Nazi who somehow got forgiven, Tim told me. This Schwartzkopf was with Bernie Dreyfus, and I saw Tim was very chummy with him. Rosey and I both remarked that Nikos would blow his stack if he knew Tim was playing footsie with this Schwartzkopf, or even Bernie Dreyfus. We mentioned it to Tim as we were driving home from the party in a taxi. Tim looked kind of sick when we brought it up.

" 'Be a couple of good kids and forget it,' he said. 'Nikos has his peculiarities. We're living in a new world, not back in the days of occupied France. Schwartzkopf is one of the biggest financial powers in Europe. Between us I've been dealing with him—for Nikos. He's made Nikos more money than you could dream. But if Nikos knew, he'd have me drawn and quartered, even though I've been doing something very much to his advantage.

"It sounded reasonable. I knew Nikos and so did Rosey. Tim was his financial adviser in a way, and he'd always made sound decisions. Nikos always said that. After Tim left us, Rosey made a kind of bitter remark to me. 'Tim isn't waiting for Nikos to die,' she said. 'He's setting up his own power complex for when it's all his.'

" 'Should we tell Nikos?' I asked her.

" 'It's Tim's party,' she said. 'He's making money for Nikos —as if he needed it! Nikos is a little old-hat.'

"So neither of us ever said anything about it. Then, this afternoon, when I realized what had happened to Nikos's pills, I began to wonder if Nikos was about to find out about Schwartzkopf and Tim's dealings with him somehow. Tim couldn't let that happen, you see. Nikos would have cut him off; it would have cost Tim millions of dollars. Then, when Rosey was found, I realized she might have thought along the same lines I was thinking and faced Tim with it. I was scared to death, Mark. I'd taken Mike Faraday away from you, but I was scared to go back to the hotel. So I came out here. I called you and they told me you and Mr. Chambrun had left the hotel. When I tried again the phone was out of order. So—so I told George Pappas everything, and he went ashore to find you and tell you. Only—"

"Only he told Tim instead," I said. I gave her the rundown on the sellout of Max Lazar's line. "Dreyfus must have threatened to tell Nikos about Schwartzkopf. Gallivan had to play ball with him, and he had to take care of Nikos because either way his goose was cooked. Then, when Rosey faced him with it, he had to take care of her. You'd be next on the list, except he has a yen for you. Apparently your Captain Pappas decided there was a rich gravy in it for him if he played along with Tim."

"But he hasn't forced me to stay here!" Jan said.

"Have you tried to go?"

"No, because I thought—"

"Well, let's try," I said.

A light flickered a few yards away in the darkness—a cigarette lighter. I saw the handsome face of Captain Pappas.

"Don't try," he said. The flame disappeared, and all I could see was the red end of his cigarette.

"George! You've double-crossed Nikos!" Jan said.

"Mr. Karados is dead," Pappas said in his deep, accented voice.

"So your bread is buttered on Gallivan's side of the street," I said.

"One must be practical," Pappas said, the red end of his cigarette bobbing up and down as he spoke.

"It isn't going to work," I said, trying to sound calm and collected. "They've got enough on Gallivan now, I think, to close in. There won't be any payoff, Captain. He won't inherit anything from Karados now."

Pappas chuckled. "There's been plenty siphoned off through the years," he said, "safely salted away in Swiss bank accounts. Once we are outside the territorial waters of the United States, we go to where no one cares. And we live. You'd better plan to get used to it, Miss Morse. Tim has a liking for you."

"And where do I fit into this future?" I asked.

"I regret to say your future will come to an end somewhere at sea, Mr. Haskell. You should have been advised not to meddle in other people's business."

"They know I'm here on the yacht," I said.

"It won't matter what they know, once we're twelve miles out," Pappas said. "Listen."

I could hear the hum of diesel engines, and a faint vibration under my feet.

"We're weighing anchor now," Pappas said.

"Going without Gallivan?"

"We pick him up down the harbor. They'd look for him here when he turns up missing. The details are all perfectly arranged. I'm sorry for you both, but I have to think of myself."

The little red circle started to move away, and then turned back. "I have a man watching from the top deck with a machine gun. If you have any heroic notions about going over the side, just know that you'll be chopped to pieces."

He was a huge man, but his tread on the deck was catlike in its silence. I looked at the shoreline. We were moving slowly down the river. No one but night owls would see us going, and all they would see would be the ship's lights. We would attract no attention. There was no way to stand at the rail and wave at someone for help. The moon had already dipped down below the Palisades, and the river was as dark as the inside of your hat. The intermittent city lights seemed like weak little blobs in the distance.

Jan clung to me, her body shaking. "It can't be real!" she whispered.

It was clear enough that the ship-to-shore phone had simply been switched off at this end. Gallivan already knew that I was aboard. He must also know that there was no point in his wasting time trying to talk Lazar into changing his mind. The time had come for him to put an escape plan into action. He would have slipped out of the hotel and headed for some predetermined escape point at the foot of Manhattan Island where he must have a boat waiting to bring him out to the *Merina*. While Chambrun and Hardy scurried around the corridors of the Beaumont looking for him, Gallivan would come aboard and the yacht's powerful engines would take us out to sea before any sort of help could take shape.

"Isn't there anything we can do, Mark?" Jan asked.

I think I've already indicated that I'm not a man of action. I've never climbed mountains, so to speak. I was too young for the Korean war and too old for Vietnam. I've never confronted anyone in my life with a weapon. Heroics are not and never have been my pattern. I'm a nice, polite young man approaching middle age who knows how to make a good dry martini and has a reasonable equipment in the way of small talk and a seven handicap at golf. Greek pirates—and that's what Pappas and his men really were—were a long way from being people I knew how to handle. But I had nothing to lose by trying something. Twelve miles out and I was going overboard with an anchor tied to my feet.

But what?

The *Merina* was sliding, swiftly now, down past the West Side Piers. I began to have a succession of crazy ideas. If I could set the ship on fire, it would attract attention. If I could somehow get to the engine room and literally throw a monkey wrench in the works, it could stop our reaching the pickup point for Gallivan.

"Where is the ship-to-shore phone?" I asked Jan. "It sounds crazy, but the most sensible thing would be to put in a call for help."

"There are phones in most of the master staterooms," Jan said. "But the main control center is in the wireless cabin, which is next to the wheelhouse on the top deck. The wireless operator would be there now."

"I understand there are all kinds of weapons on board. Do you know where they're kept?"

"There's a sort of game room forward," Jan said. "There's a ping-pong table and other things. And there's a series of locked cupboards. Nikos opened them once to show a guest. There were all kinds of guns, underwater gear, fishing knives."

"How do I get there?"

"Through the first companionway on the starboard side and then as far forward along the inside corridor as you can go."

"Now listen," I said. "It's the wildest kind of a chance, but so help me, it's the only one I can think of. You go down to your cabin and sit by the phone. I'll try to get myself some kind of weapon and go up to the wireless cabin. There I'll try to force the wireless operator to open the phone line. You call Chambrun for help."

"Mark, Pappas isn't careless. You'll never get away with it."

"You got a better idea?"

I was conscious of her warm breath, of her lips against my cheek. "Oh, God, Mark, I'm sorry I got you into this," she said. Then she took my hand. "This way," she said.

We walked together to the companionway and down about three steps into the interior of the ship.

"My cabin's at the rear," she said. "Number two. The game room is straight forward. Good luck, Mark."

I knew I was going to need it, and I had the fateful feeling it wasn't going to be forthcoming. I walked quickly to the end of the passage and opened the door in front of me. The game room was relatively large, and I instantly saw the row of paneled lockers facing me. I hadn't taken a step toward them when a door at the far end opened and a white-coated steward appeared. He gave me a toothpaste smile.

"Can I get you something, sir?"

"No, thank you," I said.

"A drink, perhaps, sir?"

"No, thank you."

He nodded, and then, God help me, he went over to the little service bar in the corner and sat down on a stool. So much for my chances of getting myself a weapon. I turned and walked back down the passage and up the companionway to the deck again. Off to the left I could see the outline of some familiar Wall Street skyscrapers. We were getting to the foot of the island, the city. I heard a distant bell and became aware of the ship slowing down. It had to be now or never. I climbed the iron stairway to the top deck. Forward I caught a glimpse of the giant figure of Pappas, standing in the glassed-in wheelhouse. I was face to face with the door of the wireless cabin. I turned the doorknob and went in.

A dark young man in a blue uniform was sitting by the wireless equipment. Just to the right of him I saw the ship-to-shore phone, with a series of switchboard connections. He, too, had a toothpaste smile. He lifted up his right hand and in it was a very serviceable-looking gun.

"Sorry, you can't come in here, sir," he said, and he meant it. He flipped a switch with his left hand and Pappas's voice came over the intercom system.

"Yes, Aristo?"

"Your male guest is visiting me, Captain."

"Thank you, Aristo."

I was thinking what my chances would be of rushing the wireless man, gun or no gun, when the door opened behind me and Pappas and a seaman came in.

"This is off limits, Mr. Haskell," Pappas said. "Anyhow, you're just in time to welcome the owner on board. This way, please."

So much for the All-American boy's heroics.

We went out onto the top deck. The seaman went down the iron ladder to the main deck and Pappas signaled me to follow him. He came down behind me.

I realized the yacht's engines were silent, and we were drifting, slowly, downstream. Coming from the shore, headed straight for us, was a little power boat. A man sat in the rear at the controls, and I saw the raincoated and hatted figure of Gallivan in the bow. I turned away, feeling sick at my stomach. Everything was working perfectly for them.

The little boat came alongside and I heard the seaman shout something to the pilot of the small boat. Someone was throwing out a line.

"Come on, Tim, shake a leg!" Pappas shouted over the side.

I turned back to watch. The hat and raincoat appeared above the rail and the seaman helped Gallivan onto the deck.

Only it wasn't Gallivan.

"Good evening, Captain Pappas," Pierre Chambrun said. He looked at what must have been my pea-green face and smiled. " 'Miss Otis regrets—' " he said.

Pappas looked as if he'd been turned to stone.

"Just bearing down on you from overhead, Captain, is a police helicopter," Chambrun said. "Coming up the harbor from Staten Island is a Coast Guard cutter. Knowing your preparedness to fight off a boarding party, it seemed my coming in advance of the authorities was the best way to avoid bloodshed on both sides. Gallivan has had it. We convinced him he was in enough trouble without bringing harm to Miss Morse and Mr. Haskell. The girl is all right, Mark?"

I nodded. My voice had disappeared somewhere.

"Bernard Dreyfus was suddenly a very frightened man," Chambrun said. His smile was grim. "He remembered me from the black days of the Resistance. When I threatened to cut out his heart, he believed me. We managed to nab Gallivan just as he was leaving the hotel by way of the kitchens. Once the harpoon was in him, the floodgates of confession opened wide. You know about his dealings with former

Nazis, Mark?"

Again I nodded.

"I suppose Miss Morse would tell you," Chambrun said. He turned to the Captain. "So far as I know, Pappas, you've not yet harmed anyone. Just taken orders. If you choose to be a cooperative witness against Gallivan, it's just possible we might forget a kidnaping charge against you."

Pappas looked wilted. "Where do you want me to take you, sir?"

"Back to your Seventy-third Street mooring," Chambrun said. He put a reassuring hand on my shoulder. "What was it Gallivan said to you, Mark? 'Sooner or later, no matter how decent his intentions, man is corrupted by his private sickness —drink, drugs, sexual deviation.' He left out his own private sickness in that catalogue—a lust for power. He had been a good friend to Nikos, a sound financial adviser. But his lust for power did him in. Schwartzkopf took him to the mountaintop and showed him the whole world. He knew how Nikos would react, and so—" Chambrun shrugged. "I think you should find your Miss Morse and tell her she can put away her track shoes. Gallivan's chasing days are over."

I turned to go.

"Oh, an unrelated fact, Mark," Chambrun said. "There was a cable for you. It seems your girl Shelda couldn't wait another ten days to tell you how she feels. She arrives at Kennedy in the morning." He chuckled. "The world is full of choices, friend. Yours seem rather delectable to a middle-aged hotel manager."

He turned to the rail to watch the Coast Guard cutter coming up the North River.